BEING OF

TWO

MINDS

BOOKS BY PAMELA F. SERVICE

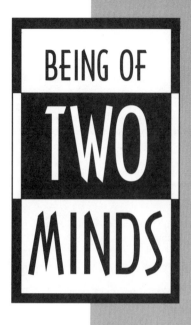

BEING OF TWO MINDS

PAMELA F. SERVICE

A Jean Karl Book

ATHENEUM · 1991 · NEW YORK
Maxwell Macmillan Canada
TORONTO
Maxwell Macmillan International
NEW YORK OXFORD SINGAPORE SYDNEY

Atheneum
Macmillan Publishing Company
866 Third Avenue
New York, NY 10022

Maxwell Macmillan Canada, Inc.
1200 Eglinton Avenue East
Suite 200
Don Mills, Ontario M3C 3N1

LIBRARY OF CONGRESS CATALOGING-IN-PUBLICATION DATA

Service, Pamela F.
  Being of two minds / Pamela F. Service.
    p.   cm.
  "A Jean Karl book."
  Summary: Connie's ability to share "mental visits" with the prince
of Thulgaria proves useful when he's mysteriously kidnapped.
  ISBN 0-689-31524-4
  [1. Extrasensory perception—Fiction.   2. Kings, queens, rulers,
etc.—Fiction.]   I. Title.
PZ7.S4885Be   1991
[Fic]—dc20   90-24097

First edition

Printed in the United States of America

Printed in Hong Kong by South China Printing Company (1988) Ltd.

Printed in

1 2 3 4 5 6 7 8 9 10

Book design by Patrice Fodero

for Katy and Lisa

CHAPTER

1

Connie Hendricks sat on the hard, cold examining table, as miserable as she had ever been in her fourteen years. It wasn't that she felt sick. She probably didn't feel anywhere near as bad as most of the people she'd seen in the hospital waiting room. It wasn't even that the thin paper smock they'd given her wouldn't stay closed, let alone keep out the cold, sterile hospital air. The problem was the fear—the fear that this time a doctor might find out what was wrong—and cure her.

She didn't want to be cured. She had lived with this all of her life. It was part of what made her *her*.

Of course, she admitted, it was awkward when she had one of her spells at school or out in public and she had only a short time to find somewhere to lie down before she fell down. But that was just the way life was for her, and she'd come to accept it.

The problem was, most other people had not accepted it. They treated her like a freak or some weird

1

space alien. Not that they were mean, usually. They were polite and friendly enough—but not too friendly. Even classmates she'd known for years acted as if her strange spells were contagious, or as if by talking with her for too long they were more likely to be around when one of the spells hit her.

At times she did wish she had close friends and led a normal life. But she didn't wish it enough to give up what she had. This specialness was precious to her, all the more so because its true nature was secret.

A clean, blank-looking nurse whisked into the room, stuck a thermometer under Connie's tongue, then whisked out again. Connie's mother gave her a supposedly reassuring smile, but Connie was not reassured. She wanted to clutch the paper dress tightly around her, run down the corridors, burst through the big double doors, and be out of there.

Of course, this doctor probably wouldn't be any more successful than all of the others. But then he was a fancy Chicago specialist and very much more expensive. He just might find out her secret.

Connie shuddered, then suddenly tightened all over as the doctor walked in. He was gray-haired, crinkly-eyed, and terribly efficient-looking. The nurse swept in behind him and removed the thermometer.

Staring down at her clenched hands, Connie listened as the doctor and her mother talked about her as if she weren't even in the room. How long had she had these spells? How often did they come? What was she like during them? He flipped through some papers and charts, then asked more questions.

Why doesn't he speak to me? Connie thought. I do speak English, you know. Then the doctor did turn to her, and Connie wished he hadn't.

Switching on a cheery smile and a kindergarten teacher voice, he said, "Now Connie dear, let's tell me about these little episodes of yours, shall we? Just what do you feel like when one of these things starts coming on?"

Careful, Connie told herself. Tell him enough to be believable, but not too much. She had played this game before, but it always scared her.

"Well, I start to feel odd, like my mind is getting kind of stretched and thin. Then I know I have maybe a minute or two to go lie down somewhere."

"Then what happens, Connie?"

"Things keep feeling thinner and tighter until they just switch off. Then when I wake up, a few hours later maybe, the feelings kind of work in reverse until everything's normal again."

"Ah, I see. And tell me, Connie, what do you feel or see or hear while you are unconscious? What seems to happen to you?"

"Nothing." She looked at the doctor with studied innocence, praying he'd believe her. "It's just like I'm really deeply asleep."

"Never any dreams?"

"Never."

"Well, well. That's all the questions for the moment, then. Let's get you hooked up to this machine and see what it tells us, shall we? It won't hurt a bit."

Tensely Connie stretched out on the thinly padded metal table. The nurse moved in on her like a vulture. She'd gone through this before, of course, and the doctor wasn't exactly lying. It didn't really hurt much. The little electrodes the nurse was attaching to her head were cold and made her feel like something out of a monster movie, and the slimy cream was cold and nasty smelling. It would take hours to scrub it out of her long blond hair. But there wasn't really much in the way of pain.

Connie lay still, trying to ignore the whole thing, trying to tune out the busy nurse and the doctor, standing halfway across the room behind his bank of space-age looking instruments. She also tried to ignore the unnatural medicinal smell and imagine in its place freshly mown grass, or maybe popcorn, buttery and hot, at a movie theater.

She failed. Fear kept slashing at imagination, dragging her back into the cold, clean, threatening hospital.

The nurse finished preparing her, and with a few falsely cheerful words, the doctor switched on the machine. Connie knew it was reading her brain waves now, but she didn't feel much of anything. The only sounds were a faint hum and the scratching and occasional click of the pencil things tracing out their patterns.

After a while, it all got more boring than frightening. Maybe now her imagination could come up with something diverting until the doctor finally gave up and admitted, like the others had done, that there was nothing abnormal about her brain waves.

Connie was deciding what story to tell herself when it struck. That telltale feeling. Usually she welcomed it, but now she felt near panic. No! she wanted to yell. Not now! The doctor may find out!

It did no good. She'd tried before, but she could never control it. These spells came at their own convenience, never at hers—nor at *his*.

The thinning, stretching feeling began to take over. The hospital room looked pale and taut, like a scene reflected in a bubble. There was nothing she could do about it now. She'd just have to let go and hope that the doctor didn't learn too much. At least not enough to cure her.

CHAPTER

2

For a moment, Rudy lost track of what his tutor was saying. The familiar dizziness hit him in a tingling wave. Then it ebbed away and he knew *she* was with him. It was never as bad at this end as when he was having one of his own spells. Then there'd be that minute or so of warning, that feeling of tightness as if the world around him were painted on a sheet of plastic and being stretched on all sides. And then, of course, he would pass out. But for now it was her turn.

"Your Highness?"

Rudy looked across the study table. His tutor raised a pale eyebrow in a worried look that showed he hadn't missed that moment of dizzy swaying.

Rudy smiled reassuringly. "I'm sorry, Wolfie. What were you saying?"

As Wolfgang Reichmann nodded, resuming his discussion of *Hamlet*, Rudy warmed with gratitude. Wolfie was the only one who took his condition in

6

stride, helping him at the beginning of his big spells, ignoring his little ones, and not making much of either afterward. If he ever told anyone the truth about them, Rudy knew it would probably be Wolfie, the young man whose pale, sparse mustache and blinking near-sighted eyes made him look more like a rodent emerging from its hole than any sort of wolf.

As his tutor pattered on, Rudy settled in with his familiar mental visitor. He hoped that wherever her unconscious body was lying at the moment, her leaving it just then hadn't been too inconvenient. They'd experimented often enough, trying to gain some control, but it had never worked very well. The books on ESP hadn't helped much either. Most of it sounded pretty faky. Whatever the exact scientific explanation, all he knew was that Connie would have to spend a while now with her mind moved in beside his. She'd retain her own identity, a presence he could feel even now, but she would be looking out of his eyes and hearing through his ears. Which reminded him of the lesson. He'd better concentrate on what Wolfie was saying.

". . . a never-ending source of satisfaction to me that you have become so fluent in English. Of course, any writer is better when read in his original language, but Shakespeare in particular seems to lose something when translated into German or anything else. It's because his prose is so close to poetry, I think. Take this passage we've been studying, or even the one line 'There are more things in heaven and earth, Horatio, than are dreamt of in your philosophy.' It's quite simple and straightforward, yet it still loses some of its flow and rhythm when we put it into German."

"Do you believe that, Wolfie?" the prince asked.

The tutor blinked several times behind his thick glasses. "Believe that Shakespeare loses rhythm in translation?"

"No, what the words are saying. That 'there are more things in heaven and earth' et cetera."

The young man thoughtfully tugged his mustache. "Yes, I believe I do. Shakespeare had a knack for hitting the nail on the head even four hundred years ago. Substitute the word 'science' for 'philosophy,' and it applies today. There are things out there that all the computers and scientists in the world can't explain." He let a look of theatrical alarm sweep over his face, then wagged a finger. "Now don't you go telling the king that I believe in pyramid power and UFOs or I'll be out of the royal household faster than you can say 'bigfoot.'"

Rudy laughed. "But I'm sure Father appreciates open minds." His smile flickered into seriousness. "And I certainly do." He wondered if Wolfie threw ESP into the same bag as UFOs.

"Hmm, yes," the other said glancing at the ornate bronze clock squatting on the mantel. "And one of the problems with an open mind is that it makes me so easy to lead off the subject at hand. But we'd better let Hamlet rest for a while since you'll have to be getting ready soon for tonight's state reception."

Rudy was relieved. He'd been having these mental visits since he was a baby and never felt the need to act like a tour guide during them. Still it seemed a shame if the whole time she was with him was to be taken up with something like lessons. It had happened before. He stood up.

"I'd almost forgotten about that. Who is it tonight, anyway? The Russian ambassador, or is it the American?"

"Neither. Tonight's the Romanian."

"Oh yes, the one who looks like a bald ostrich."

Wolfie's eyes twinkled." Now, Your Highness, is that any way to . . ."

Rudy laughed and headed to the door. "Don't worry, your instructions have been absorbed. Future kings of Thulgaria are to keep their observations about ambassadors looking like bald ostriches strictly to themselves."

Rudy walked jauntily from the upstairs study and headed toward the top of the sweeping marble staircase. It had been raining for two days, and now that the sun was out he was determined to spend these few minutes of freedom outside. Besides, there were some late pears ripe in the orchard just now. It was a pity his mental friend couldn't taste the food he ate while she was visiting, but at least she'd enjoy the tree climbing, particularly since they both knew that such activities were discouraged for dignified royal princes.

Happily he trotted down the red carpet that flowed down the center of the marble stairs. The late afternoon sun streaming through the French windows set the polished wood of the parquet floor glowing with light. Rudy smiled, remembering how when he was little he'd spend hours hopping between patterns of dark and light wood. But now he strode across them and out the doors.

Standing by the stone balustrade, he looked out over the palace gardens. Everything glowed with fresh autumn colors as tier on tier of formal flowerbeds, fountains, and sweeping tree-dotted lawns spread off in all directions. From below, there rose scattered bird songs, and the less tuneful trilling of Princess Charlotte. Somewhere down there, his plump six-year-old sister was running the royal nanny ragged after days of confinement by the rain. Good thing, Rudy thought, that the orchards were in the other direction.

He turned toward the eastern stairs then stopped when he saw the dark slender figure climbing toward him: Duke Albrecht. Rudy smiled inside and out. If there was one person he really felt at ease with, besides Wolfie, it was Uncle Albrecht. His uncle was fun. Of course, Rudy loved and respected his father; but being king, his father didn't have much time to spend with his family. Occasionally he took his son golfing with him or on royal functions, but Rudy wasn't too excited by either. Albrecht, however, took his nephew to movies, museums, or hiking in the woods. Or they'd just talk.

Albrecht had a clever irreverant way of looking at everything, even politics and the royal family. Rudy didn't think he always agreed with Albrecht, but listening to him was like listening to one of those reprehensively witty comedians. Rudy wondered whether he'd ever seem as charming and clever as his uncle or just be dull and sincere like his father.

Looking casually rakish in his black turtleneck and white slacks, Albrecht climbed the last few steps and fixed Rudy with his wry smile. "Ah, glad to see you've broken out into the fresh air. Got to watch your health, you know."

Rudy nodded tautly. That was Albrecht's big fault: his concern about his nephew's health. Of course, it was nice of him to be concerned, and really it wasn't much different from Connie's relatives. The first thing they seemed to associate with her was poor health, as if she were some frail invalid with nothing else to talk about. Maybe he could turn the conversation in some other direction.

"Uncle, are you going to the reception tonight for the Romanian ambassador?"

"Yes, and I can't imagine what's gotten into me. Here I left my lovely little chateau just to stay in this architectural monstrosity and attend this boring send-off for that boring scrawny-necked old Romanian."

"Ah, but there'll be all those exciting speeches." Rudy smiled what he hoped was a clever sarcastic smile.

Albrecht rolled his eyes. "Ah yes, the speeches. The Romanian mumbles, so we'll be spared most of him, but your father . . . With all due respect to my esteemed big brother, I can almost hear the king's speech now. 'My friends and most honored neighbors of our ancient realm of Thulgaria . . .' "

Rudy had to fight an ear-to-ear grin. Albrecht did a very good imitation of his brother's flat tone and flowery words. Rudy hated to admit it, but his father was a dreadful public speaker.

"Our kingdom is like a rock," Albrecht continued in mimicry. "Others bow and bend in the winds of history like trees or grass. Yet when the fires come, they are consumed. But we, like the rocks, are unmoving. We remain!"

Rudy gave in to a giggle. Albrecht had captured it exactly.

"Right!" Albrecht said emphatically. "It *is* rubbish."

"Oh, I don't know," Rudy said, partly from loyalty and partly from conviction. "The speaking style sure is, but not the words really. I'm told Grandpa always said the same when he was king."

"Exactly. And your father is just as outdated. Come now, no one knows and loves my brother better than I, but you must admit he's a bit of an old fuddy.

12

Now you and I, Rudolph, are of a different generation. We can see that the only way to survive over time is to change. Trees may sway with the breeze, but at least they don't get trampled on the way rocks do. And they can always sway the other way when the breeze changes."

Rudy had to admit Uncle Albrecht sounded pretty convincing. He always did. But somehow when you thought about what he said, the arguments didn't ring quite true. From everything Wolfie had taught him about Thulgarian history, it seemed the only thing that allowed their tiny kingdom to survive was strict political and economic neutrality: never siding with any other country no matter how big and powerful; never forming alliances; never joining wars. Now and again they did get invaded, but even then they wouldn't cooperate, and in the end they'd always come up free again.

Finally Rudy shook his head. "I know what you're saying, but I really can't agree, not with all of it. Neutrality may be dull, but it's safe."

"Good lord, another old fuddy—and at age fourteen! Come on boy, someday you'll be king of this place. We'll need someone fit to lead us into the next millennium, not into a regurgitated history lesson."

That last comment stung like a whip. Rudy knew he shouldn't be so sensitive about references to his health, but he couldn't help it. "I *am* fit! It's all right for *some* people to play games with the Russians or the

Americans or the Germans or whoever is blowing hardest at the moment—even to suggest that we bend with them and join some economic pact or political alliance. But as you said, I'm the one who has to be king someday, *which I am perfectly fit to be,* and I don't want to see Thulgaria blown down while I am."

Albrecht shot his nephew a sharp look that melted into concern. "Sorry kid, I shouldn't let you get upset like that. You all right?"

"Of course I'm all right!" Immediately Rudy was sorry he'd snapped back. Albrecht wouldn't know that anger couldn't bring on his spells. "Sorry, but I really do think your ideas are a little off the mark."

Albrecht smiled ruefully. "As I think yours are. Can't understand it. All my years of black-sheep tutelage and you get to sound more like my brother every day. But maybe after one more dose of it tonight, you'll have a blinding revelation and see through all the claptrap."

He glanced at his watch then back at the prince. "And it's about time we both made ourselves ready for the ordeal. It sounds like the princess has already been dragged off to her bath. The garden is blissfully quiet."

When Albrecht had hurried off, Rudy cast a regretful glance toward the pear orchard then shrugged and walked slowly back to the palace and up the stairs. Halfway to his room, a smile began twitching about his lips. What would Uncle Albrecht say if he knew

14

that a stranger had been sitting in on their little family quarrel? The thought lifted his depression over the quarrel itself.

Of course, Connie was hardly a stranger. On and off, she'd been part of his family since he'd been born, just as he'd been part of hers. In the beginning he hadn't disguised it, assuming that everyone made and received such visits. He talked about it like any other event. But even a toddler can tell when he's saying something that no one believes or wants to hear. The same, of course, had happened to Connie until it became their shared secret.

And at times he wished that they shared more. Their attempts at picking up actual thoughts had always failed, though they'd used experiments suggested in books as well as ones they'd designed themselves. Right now he'd really like to know what she thought of Albrecht's arguments. But, although he felt her presence, her mind had only moved in *beside* his, not into it. Still, it seemed that, as people, they had a lot in common. When he was with Connie in her life, she responded to things a lot the way he would. And they'd found some ways to communicate. He'd try one now.

Checking to see no one else was in the hall, he said out loud, "Well, what do you think? Is Uncle Albrecht right, or is my father? Not that it would matter to most people who aren't history professors or future kings, but . . ."

15

A maid popped out of a room ahead, and he shut up, turning quickly into his own room.

His clothes for the evening had already been laid out on his bed. He curled his lip. The stiff formal reception outfit. He envied Connie and her fellows being able to live in jeans and T-shirts. Well, at least he didn't have to deal with a flock of servants helping him dress the way royalty had in the old days.

Mechanically he undressed then put on the white military-looking suit, draping the broad gold sash across his chest. He scarcely thought about the fact that there was a girl inside his mind while he did this. He'd been inside her mind as often at such times, and as far as he was concerned, they were almost two forms of the same person.

Not that they looked alike, he thought glancing at a mirror. With his straight nose and curly black hair, he hardly looked like the twin of the person he saw in *her* mirror, an American girl with a pug nose and straight blond hair. But their minds were as good as twins, and had been since the moment, the very same moment, that they had been born.

Of course, once they had realized the uniqueness of their situation, both had tried to understand its cause. But beyond a shared moment of birth, and possibly a very distant genetic link through Connie's Thulgarian great-grandparents, there didn't seem to be an obvious explanation. The ESP books that Connie had read helped only a little. They talked about similar mental patterns seeking each other out and being transmitted almost like sound. To really understand that, Rudy figured one of them would have to become an electrical engineer. After a while they'd quit trying to find an explanation. If what happened couldn't be explained, then maybe it couldn't be stopped either. And neither of them wanted it stopped.

The muffled throb of a gong from downstairs startled Rudy back to the present. The reception was beginning. He ran a comb through his hair with little noticeable effect, then after pausing a few minutes to finish a comic book he'd gotten Wolfie to smuggle in, he headed reluctantly downstairs.

Already the hall was filling up, and some people in the formally dressed crowd were spilling out onto the terrace, enjoying the fine autumn evening. Outside, the light from lamps and a low half-moon was soft and cool, casting blue shadows among the poplars, willows, and pines. Inside, however, the palace was ablaze with light. Floor-to-ceiling mirrors along two walls reflected not only themselves but everything in between: the crystal chandeliers, the sparkling jewels on the guests, and the gold leaf adorning walls and furniture. In one corner, a chamber quartet sent music drifting among the chattering, laughing guests.

His parents, Rudy saw, had already made their entrance. The king's white uniform, bedecked with sash, medals, and tassled gold epaulets, was a very ornate version of Rudy's own. Even so, he was quite outshone by the queen whose green satin gown matched the emeralds gleaming on her ample chest.

The royal couple was chatting with the retiring Romanian ambassador, who, Rudy noted again, looked very much like a bald ostrich. The big man next to him was probably his replacement, who, being large and hairy with little close-set eyes, looked more like a bear than any kind of bird.

Catching his eye, Rudy's mother motioned for him to join them. He was introduced and shook their hands in turn, first the birdlike talon, then the crushing bear paw. Trying not to wince, Rudy wondered if the bones in his hand would ever find their right alignment again. His father threw him a fleeting glance, a smile twitching up a corner of his short gray beard. Obviously his hand was suffering the same. The king resumed his discussion with the ambassadors on the politically neutral subject of the latest joint space venture by the Russians and the Americans.

After several minutes of stiff, polite talk, Rudy excused himself and drifted off after a servant balancing a silver tray of hors d'oeuvres. If he could make enough of a meal here, maybe he could skip the formal dinner afterward, though he suspected his parents would notice and object. He hated these dinners and much preferred meals at Connie's house. Not that he could taste anything since somehow the senses of taste and smell didn't seem to be part of this link. Different parts of the brain, maybe. But he liked the casual convenience of passing food around and serving one's self, and of sitting at a small table chatting about the day's events, or even eating on little folding trays in front of the television. Still, he supposed Connie was enjoying this experience as much as he did the other. He decided to make a point of looking in every direction, like a scanning camera, so she could see it all.

In one of his sweeps he caught his uncle's dark eyes upon him, and blushing, he immediately looked down. Albrecht was a pretty easy going guy, but Rudy didn't want him noticing his odd "sickly" nephew acting as if he were seeing everything in his home for the first time. Rudy shot the Duke what he hoped was a jaunty smile and deliberately walked over to join Princess Charlotte. She had one of the waiters bending down so she could decide which of the little fancily shaped sandwiches she'd try next. From the smudges on her plump cheeks, Rudy decided she'd already tried quite a few.

He was just suggesting she try one with salmon paste shaped like a rose when the wave of dizziness hit and he felt Connie's presence slip away from him. He staggered back a step, and Charlotte looked up at him matter-of-factly.

"Don't fall down now, Rudy. You'll miss dinner and there's chocolate mousse for dessert."

When his vision cleared, Rudy smiled at her weakly then realized there was a steadying hand on his arm. He looked around and his eyes met Uncle Albrecht's, his expression sharply concerned.

"You all right, kid? That brother and sister-in-law of mine shouldn't make you come to ghastly affairs like this when you're not up to it."

Feelings ripped through Rudy like tides going in opposite directions. Of course he'd love to get out of these dreary events, but *not* because he wasn't up to them. How could Albrecht see one fact and not the other?

He straightened up. "I'm all right, Uncle. This party may be a bore, but I'm perfectly up to it, thanks."

Calmly he selected a sandwich and walked away eating it. He wished that Connie had not left just then, and not simply because his dizziness had been seen. It was good not to always be alone.

CHAPTER 3

Connie felt herself snapping back as if she were a ball on the end of an elastic string. The usual regret rose around her as it does when one awakes too soon from an interesting dream. Only, unlike a dream, this wouldn't fade. It had all happened in the real world somewhere. She'd remember it as clearly as anything she'd done herself.

Herself! Fear burst up, flooding out the regret. What an awful time for this to have happened!

"I think she's coming out of it now." Her mother's voice sounded near. Connie opened her eyes to see her mother and the nurse smiling reassuringly at her. Again she was not reassured. What had they learned? The doctor was talking to a colleague on the other side of his instrument console. Connie strained to listen.

"Well, that's it, then. An absolutely normal reading again. The most remarkable thing I've ever seen."

"How long did it last?"

The first doctor glanced at a screen. "One hundred and thirty seven minutes."

"And the only identifiable abnormalities were where?"

There was a rustle of paper. "Here and here. Points where the seizure was beginning and ending. All the readings go haywire for a second or two, though not in any manner I've seen before. Then they settle back to normal."

"Except for this, of course."

"Yes, that's just it. Except for this incredible echo. It's almost as if the machine were hooked up to two brains at once."

"Hmm, yes. But these two patterns are almost identical. Surely there's just some glitch in the machine and it's tracing a duplicate pattern."

"That's what I thought at first, but I had plenty of time to check the equipment out. It's functioning perfectly. And besides, the patterns aren't quite identical. See this spike here or those there? It's as though we were recording two separate individuals, but ones whose brain waves were even more alike than twins. Not that it's statistically possible for two brains to be that alike, or to be recorded at the same time, for that matter. But that is the impression it gives."

Connie's mother joined the two doctors, and they went on talking while the nurse busied herself removing the electrodes and scrubbing the worst of the goo out of Connie's hair. She couldn't follow all the medical conversation, but the more she heard, the better Connie felt.

Was that what happened then? "Statistically impossible" or not, her mind and Rudy's mind were so alike that they kept slipping in and out of each other? Wonderful, she thought at the doctors. Go ahead and think it's a glitch in the machine. Her secret felt warm and safe inside her.

Finally the puzzled doctors let them go, but before they began their drive home, Connie persuaded her mother to stop at the Chicago Public Library so she could check out some books not available at home. Her father, she pointed out, could return them on one of his frequent trips into Chicago.

When her mother saw Connie staggering out under a stack of thick scholarly looking books, she shook her head. "Let me guess. Thulgaria. The Midwest's Thulgarian fanatic has just cleaned out the Chicago Library."

Connie smiled tolerantly, stacking her treasures on the floor of the car.

Mrs. Hendricks shrugged and started up the station wagon. She ought to be used to this by now, she told herself. Her daughter had been interested in that obscure little Central European country for as long as she could remember. At some impressionable age she must have heard mention of her Thulgarian great-grandparents and been obsessed ever since. Now her room was decorated from floor to ceiling with travel posters and magazine pictures showing everything from picturesque scenes and castles, to colorful dance troops and even the Thulgarian royal family.

Her mother had to admit that if Connie was going to be fanatical about something, there were worse and noisier possibilities. A rock group, for instance. There were even some benefits. Connie's interest had been so intense that she'd somehow managed to teach herself German, Thulgaria's official language, at a very early age. People who knew German said she spoke it as well as a native.

All the way home and for days afterward, Connie pored over the books. Some of them were hard going, but Rudy had asked her a question, and she was determined to have an answer for him when he next joined her.

As usual, that time came when least expected. Connie was riding home on the school bus when the tingly dizziness hit her. She swayed forward in her seat trying to ignore the nervous sidelong glances of the boy sitting next to her. It was evening in Thulgaria and she imagined Rudy, having just passed out, being carried off to an early bed with the usual hushed-up efficiency. Except that he wasn't really there at all now, but with her, riding in the crowded noisy school bus.

She looked at the boy next to her whose face was struggling between revulsion and curiosity. "I'm okay," she said, knowing full well that he hadn't been worried about her as much as about what he would do if this freaky girl passed out beside him. He'd probably seen her do it at school.

But Connie smiled. She really didn't care what that kid thought. She had a real friend with her now. Turning her attention to the window, she watched the street scene rumble by. She saw it almost every day, of course, but she didn't recall that Rudy had ever been with her on the bus. The new scenery ought to interest him, though she was sorry he hadn't been with her at track practice earlier that day. She'd come in second.

Once home, Connie grabbed a quick snack and retreated to her room. There she sat down and between bites of raisin toast, launched into an answer to Rudy's question.

"I've decided it's your father rather than your uncle who's right," she said aloud. "All through Thulgaria's history, it's tried to avoid getting entangled with other peoples. The Ostrogoths, the Huns, the Teutonic knights, all the way up to the Second World War and the cold war. And somehow it's managed to survive. Even after an invasion, the invaders would eventually leave or get absorbed and Thulgaria would pop up independent again."

Connie looked at the stack of books on her desk and shrugged. "Of course, you've probably read a whole lot more Thulgarian history than I have. But hey, two minds are better than one." Her laugh was cut short by her mother's voice outside the door.

"Connie, I've told you before, talking to yourself is not a good idea. It makes people think you're strange."

Connie's anger flared then fizzled. Poor Mom, she thought, so hung up on what people think. Why should they mind that she was odd if *she* didn't mind? Still, mothers are like that.

"It's okay, Mom, I'm just reciting the poems I'm supposed to do aloud for English."

Nevertheless Connie put the rest of her historical analysis down on paper for Rudy to read through her eyes. They'd learned that since they couldn't exchange thoughts, writing and talking aloud were the only ways to communicate directly, and then one had to wait weeks for answers. Of course, there were shared experiences too. That thought made her decide that writing history wasn't the best way to spend a visit.

Connie went downstairs, and after much coaxing, persuaded her mother to take her to the movies in the mall for the cheap late afternoon showing. Her mother didn't like her going places alone for fear she might have one of her spells, but fortunately this was a movie her mother too was vaguely interested in seeing.

Rudy had been with Connie before when she'd gone to the mall and had later said how much he'd enjoyed it. But now they headed straight for the theater. The movie was a sort of medieval fantasy that started out with an old knight and his son destroying a witch. But before she evaporates, the witch curses them to "live in interesting times." The boy is delighted, figuring that now he won't have to spend his life in their dull little village; but soon a dragon attacks and everybody but the boy is killed. He wanders off, gets involved in a war between wizards, saves a beautiful shepherdess from an ogre, and nearly gets buried under an avalanche of enchanted crystals.

They were just working up to the final battle with the arch-dragon when Connie felt Rudy leave her. Poor guy, she thought. She'd be furious if someone dragged her out of the theater just before the end. When next she could, she'd have to remember to tell him how it came out.

Another week passed before they got together again, and then it was Connie who did the visiting. The tight stretchy feeling came on her while she was staying up late one night studying for a history test on the events that led up to the Civil War. This was the best possible timing, she thought, as she quickly turned off the light. All she had to do was dive into bed, and if anyone looked in on her, they wouldn't know she wasn't just sleeping normally.

She particularly hated it when the spells hit her at school. She'd have to quickly get up and run to the cold plastic couch in the nurse's office. The teachers always told the kids not to stare at her, but some did, and anyway the averted eyes were almost worse. But she didn't really mind too much as long as she made it to the office. It was embarrassing to wake up on the couch and realize that they'd had to pick her up from the hallway or the playground and carry her there.

But this was safe and private. Her darkened bedroom thinned and snapped until she was seeing a landscape that was moving past her and jolting slightly up and down. A newly risen sun was thinning a film of mist, and through it she could see the dark twisted shapes of nearly leafless trees.

When the dizziness and the sense of joining struck him, Rudy gripped the saddle to steady himself, and slowed his horse to a walk. Then as the scenery settled again, Rudy turned his bay mare down the next branching path. Though she didn't get much of a chance where she lived, he knew Connie enjoyed riding. Once, years ago, she'd written him a note about how surprised her fellow Brownies were at seeing how well she could ride at their first lesson. Of course, she couldn't tell them she'd been through several lessons with Thulgaria's royal riding instructor. To be fair, Rudy had just as good a time if, when he was with her, she and some of the neighborhood kids went skateboarding. That certainly wasn't anything he could do here, though he'd love to see people's faces if he started executing a few Ollies and McTwists in the halls or formal gardens of the palace.

The path led them to a secluded dell guarded by

ranks of dark drooping pines. The only sound was the dew dripping off the branches and the crunch of gravel under the horse's hooves. Then, with an eerie cry, a large white bird fluttered up from a silver sheet of water. Mist rising from its surface coiled around the columns of a small pearl-white temple that stood on an island in the little lake.

"This," Rudy announced into the resettling morning stillness, "is part of the Romantic Gardens that King Gustav III added to the palace grounds in the eighteenth century. Gustav didn't care whether styles were classical or oriental or medieval or what, so long as they were weird and romantic. He also added a bunch of odd stuff to our palace, and to other palaces all over the country. My favorite spot's the Grotto of Neptune."

Rudy headed the horse along the edge of the lake, all the while hoping no one else was about. Of course, he could always say that his horse liked good educational talks. Steadied her nerves.

On the far shore, the lake lapped into a shallow cave set in a cliff. In the center of the cave, a stone dolphin seemed to leap from the pool. Its back shone under the steady splash of water cascading from an urn held by a bearded stone man. He wore a crown of starfish and in his other hand clutched a three-pointed spear.

"On summer days, you can sit on the dolphin's

back and be almost hidden by the screen of water. Great place to hide."

After a time watching the splash of water into the moss green pool, Rudy sighed and headed his horse back up the path. "Ought to get back now. Sometimes they fuss about my riding out alone. And I'd better shut up since the gardeners'll be puttering about soon."

Once he'd turned his horse over to the groom at the stables Rudy, feeling famished, headed to the palace and the family breakfast room. It was smaller, lighter, and less ornate than the formal dining rooms. Rudy liked it a lot better.

A row of heated platters were set out along a sideboard keeping the food warm, but from their state of depletion it looked as if everyone else had already eaten. He was a little sorry about that. Duke Albrecht had come down again from his chateau in the north and was staying with them for a few days. There probably wouldn't be time to do anything interesting together. But even their conversations could be fun, though of late they'd tended to be heavy and political.

Rudy was just finishing a second jam-slathered croissant, and wishing yet again that taste could be shared mentally, when his sister Charlotte bounced into the room.

"There you are, Rudy. Some of them are pretty mad you went riding this morning." She crossed her pudgy arms and looked pleased with herself at having passed on this bit of information.

"Thanks for the warning, Tot. I guess I'll lay low until the fuss is over."

"Good, then you can play hide-and-seek with me."

Rudy groaned. He'd really walked into that one. But why not? He was sure to have found a lot more hiding places than Charlotte could have in her six, going on seven, years.

"Okay. What rules?"

"I'm *it*. You hide, but stay in the west wing. The rest's not fair."

"Agreed."

"I'll stay here," she said reaching for what was probably not her first sweet roll of the morning, "and count to two hundred."

"You can't count that high."

"Can too!"

"Yeah, but you don't use all the numbers in between."

"You're a meany! I can too count right."

"All right, all right. You count, and I'll hide."

She began counting between licks of icing, and Rudy sprinted out of the room. Where to hide? That's one thing about a palace, he admitted, plenty of hiding places. Under tables or behind tapestries or suits of armor would be too obvious. Charlotte was good at this. But he bet that she hadn't found all the secret

31

passages and such that the mad builder Gustav III had put in.

He hurried down a long hall where sunlight shining through stained glass splashed pools of color over the tile floor. Briefly he considered crawling into one of the giant Chinese urns outside the library door, but wasn't sure he'd be able to get out again. Instead, entering the library, he ignored the walls lined with books and walked straight to the large fireplace. Two grinning gargoyles carved in green marble were holding up the mantle. Moving to the one on the right, he reached up and twisted an ear.

With a soft click, a narrow section of paneling beside the fireplace slowly slid open. Rudy slipped in and, using a handle on the inside, closed the secret panel.

For a moment he stood still, letting his eyes get used to the dark. But it wasn't totally dark. Dusty light filtered in through a latticework of fine cracks where the carvings on the outside paneling had been deliberately cut through. There were even several larger openings, concealed as carved wooden roses, that allowed someone hidden in the wall to peer into the rooms on either side. Not that there was much to see in the library at the moment. But at least he could keep a lookout for Charlotte, and if she started getting too close, he could slip down the passage and out the panel that led into the drawing room on the other side.

Rudy couldn't decide if Great-Great-Whatever-Grandfather Gustav III had been a genius or a nut case, but his building additions were full of this sort of thing. They certainly had given generations of royal children interesting scope for play. Not a bad exchange considering that the chances for young royalty to play with other children were often pretty limited. Occasionally children of nobility had been brought in to play with him, but he'd had less of that than most princes, since officials were afraid of rumors about his health.

Rudy's musings were interrupted by voices, but peering out of a spy hole, he could see that the library was still empty. Must be from the drawing room, then. He crept along the passage and put his eye to a hole on the other side. At first he couldn't see anything except furniture, but then his mother moved into view followed by Uncle Albrecht. They seemed angry.

"Really, Catherine dear, " Albrecht was saying, "I admire your determination not to be an overprotective mother. But you're not just dealing with one woman's son, you're dealing with the heir to the throne of Thulgaria."

Rudy's interest focused from casual to intense. He wished he could see his mother's face, but from the tone of her voice he could well imagine the icy glare that went with it.

"That is the last thing I am forgetting. If he were simply my son, I'd be tempted to hold him close as long as I could and protect him from all possible harm. But he *is* the heir to the throne, and a coddled prince who is never allowed to stub his toe would make a pretty feeble king."

"But at least he wouldn't be a dead one! How could you allow him to go riding alone like that? If one of his seizures had hit him, he could have toppled off his horse and broken his neck or fallen into one of those damned ornamental pools and drowned."

"Don't imagine I don't think about that, Albrecht, every moment I'm not with him. But he does have enough warning when one of those episodes is coming to get out of any dangerous position."

"And you're willing to let him just lie unconscious out there in the gardens for hours?"

"The servants and gardeners are all alerted to that possibility."

"Yes, and they're all sworn to secrecy too, aren't they? You know, dearest sister-in-law, you can't hide the truth from the people forever. Someday they'll learn that the heir to the throne of Thulgaria is prone to uncontrollable, incapacitating seizures."

The queen sat down solidly on a couch just out of Rudy's sight. "And when they do learn it, it won't matter to them. They are loyal, and they love their royal family. They might feel sorry for him, but they won't condemn him. He's a smart, caring boy. He'll make a good king."

"Catherine, my dear, you are living in a fairy tale. Even in dear old Thulgaria there are plenty of people who feel the monarchy has outlived its usefulness. Others think we ought to abandon the old neutrality line that the royal family's been so keen on and start shopping around for the most useful international friends. They argue that as long as we're neutral, we can't play the superpowers off against each other and reap all the economic advantages they'd offer us as bait. Wake up, Catherine! More and more people are thinking that way, and seeing the royal family as a stumbling block to progress."

"And that's your opinion too, Albrecht?"

"Of course not. I'm as royal as the rest of you. But a defective royal heir would give fuel to those people."

In his hiding place, Rudy tightened all over. Defective? Surely Uncle Albrecht couldn't mean that.

"So what are you suggesting," the queen said coldly, "that we have a nursemaid stay with Rudolph night and day?"

"You could do that, but it would be better if you could find a cure for his condition."

"Albrecht, you know we have tried! Every specialist in Europe has been called in to look at him. They are baffled. Rudy says he has no idea what happens during his spells, and his EEGs are perfectly normal. The most they've turned up were some echoey ghost lines a couple of times, for which no one had an explanation. Don't you think that if we could find a cure, we would?"

"Well, bitter as it is, there is another alternative open to you."

And what is that?"

"You could remove him from the line of succession."

CHAPTER

4

Rudy felt as if a spear had been thrust into his middle. He hoped they hadn't heard his gasp from inside the wall. But in the drawing room, his mother and uncle were intent only on each other.

"Indeed," the queen said, standing and pacing slowly across the room. "And I suppose you're suggesting we name *you* heir instead."

Albrecht's laugh was like gunshot. "Not me, my dear. I'm perfectly content being a duke, the richest playboy in Europe, and totally free of all kingly obligations. I don't have the temperament to be heir or king. But Princess Charlotte seems as healthy as a horse and full of common sense. She'd make an admirable heir and queen someday."

Queen Catherine looked at him steadily. "Yes, of course. And as her beloved uncle you'd sacrifice your time to act as her confidant and adviser, even as regent should she have to come to the throne early."

37

Rudy could see that she was smiling now, but her plump face looked anything but soft and motherly. "Clever, Albrecht, how you've managed to get those two children to dote on you all these years."

"Catherine, I'm used to snide comments about my morals, but *that* is not fair. I love those kids, and I want Rudy out of harm's way. That's all! If Brother Wilhelm is so careless as to die before his time, then Parliament chooses the regent. Somehow I doubt they'd find ne'er-do-well Albrecht a fit candidate."

"You know, I really don't believe . . ."

The argument flared on, but Rudy's attention was dragged from it by a muffled click. Back along the dusky passage, the secret panel was slowly sliding open. Numbly he stumbled toward it and grabbed Charlotte by the shoulders just as she was about to hesitantly step in.

"Clever kid," he said, trying to drag lightness over his quaking feelings of anger and loss. "However did you find me?" Firmly he led her away from the passage and closed the panel.

"Easy, you weren't under or behind things, so I guessed you were in one of the secret places. Those scary gargoyle things in this part of the palace are all hiding one. Didn't you know that?"

"Yeah, but I didn't know you did."

"I know lots."

"You are pretty smart, at that." He looked down

at her sharply for a moment. "What would you think of being queen someday?"

"Don't want to. Mama and Papa have to work hard and go to all those dumb 'ceptions. I want to stay a princess, have lots of pretty dresses, and not work much. But I like hide-and-seek. Now you're it."

"No. Sorry, Tot. No more hide-and-seek for me today. I've got to . . . think. Then I've got lessons with Wolfie."

"That's dumb. Thinking and lessons. Why do you want to do that?"

"Because, goose, I've got to learn to be a king. I *want* to be king someday. And I'll be a good one too."

"Sure, go ahead and be a king if you want. Just don't make your sister go to all those dumb 'ceptions."

"*Receptions.*"

"I don't like those either."

Finally Charlotte bounded off on some other pursuit. Rudy glumly wandered out into the formal garden where the clipped hedges, tidy flower beds, and straight intersecting paths were simple and orderly. Exactly what his churning thoughts needed to be. Maybe here he could manage to be alone and think. Well, he wasn't quite alone. Now, more than ever, he wanted to be able to talk with Connie, to communicate immediately back and forth. He needed more than a comforting presence; he needed help.

Suddenly he realized he wouldn't even have that presence. The surge of dizziness sent him reeling toward a stone bench. "Don't go!" he whispered hopelessly. But she had gone. He slumped onto the bench, very much alone.

Connie opened her eyes to the darkness of her room, and abruptly sat up in bed. She wished desperately that she had been asleep just then, that it had all been a dream, a nightmare that would fade and be forgotten. But it had all been real and she had been there. Like Rudy, she needed to think about it, to get over the hurt and confusion. It wasn't until nearly dawn that she fell asleep.

In the next few days, she thought about it a great deal. Not that she came to many useful conclusions. One thing was clear, however. Things had changed and were taking a new and alarming turn.

This wasn't just her and Rudy's private secret any more—its pleasure making up for the trouble it caused. It was something that well might cause Rudy to lose the most important thing in his life: being crown prince. Of course, some kids would as soon be free of that duty and responsibility, but Rudy had expected and prepared for it all of his life, and in time, Connie thought, he would be a good king. It meant as much to her as it did to him that he have that chance.

But now it looked as if Rudy could lose his birthright because of his, of their, strange condition. She wondered if they were still right in keeping it a secret. Maybe the doctors couldn't do anything about it, but if they knew what was really happening, perhaps they could control it or at least not take it so seriously.

Yet suppose they took it even more seriously? Suppose they decided they had to study the two of them, and took them away to laboratories and treated them like freaks? Then things would be worse than they were now.

The following week, Connie had another appointment with the expensive Chicago doctor, but despite a new battery of tests, he didn't learn a thing. Several times she was tempted to tell him the truth and ask his help. But she felt that she first had to talk it over with Rudy in their awkward delayed conversations.

Through the winter they had several of these. Also, they again took up their experiments, trying to bring on these exchanges in a more convenient way. They were not particularly successful. It did seem that if each concentrated on the other person, they could maybe bring a spell on a day or so earlier, but there was still no control over timing.

In the end they decided not to tell anybody yet. Rudy was afraid that such a story might be seen as another sign he wasn't fit to be heir. Besides, it seemed that the queen and king had not been impressed with

Albrecht's arguments. It was true that there were factions in the populace and government who wanted change, who wanted leadership headed in a different direction. But the royal couple was convinced that the vast majority of people were with them and would want their son, ill or not, to remain heir.

Then in the early spring came news that drove away worries about politics, betrayed friendships, and hidden secrets. It was decided that in May the Thulgarian royal family would make a state visit to the United States. They would stop in Washington, D.C., to visit the president, and in Los Angeles to visit Disneyland and Hollywood. But in between they would also visit Chicago. This was partly because of the large Thulgarian immigrant population that had settled there in the last century. But Connie also knew that Prince Rudolph had done considerable lobbying to have them stop and "see something of middle America."

When Connie woke up on the school nurse's couch after learning that, it was all she could do to keep from blurting the news. She waited impatiently until the next morning at home, then galloped downstairs shouting, "Guess what I heard on the radio?"

"School's been canceled for today?" her father suggested.

"No, better. The Thulgarian royal family will be visiting the United States in May! And they'll be stopping in Chicago!"

"That's nice dear," Connie's mother said blandly, as she sleepily tightened the bathrobe around her thin waist.

"But Mom, if they're going to be that close, we've simply got to go there and get a peek at them."

"Connie, darling," her father said, "the family of a small town lawyer is hardly going to be invited to diplomatic receptions for foreign royalty."

"I'm not talking about formal receptions. There are bound to be times when they're out in public. I bet every bit of their schedule will be published in the newspapers. There ought to be plenty of chances for ordinary people to get a look at them."

"I fail to understand," her father said, putting down the newspaper, "this fascination for staring at celebrities. Besides, these people didn't even make themselves celebrities, they were born that way."

"Well sure, but maybe that's what makes them especially exciting. After all, there are darn few kings and queens left these days. Yet that used to be the way everything was run. Seeing them will be educational, a glimpse of ancient history."

Her mother laughed. "She's got you there, Paul."

He grunted, then brushed toast crumbs off his pot belly and stood up. "And I also fail to understand why you have developed a fixation on that dinky little country. All they do is live on tourists and stamp collectors."

"And cheese lovers," Connie added.

"All right, and cheese lovers. But most kids get worked up about rock singers or movie stars. What is it with this Thulgaria place?"

Connie was silent a moment then said, "Well, it's quieter than a rock singer and not as phony as a movie star. It's pretty, and it has really interesting history, and its people are very nice."

"How do you know? You've never seen a real Thulgarian. You never even met your Thulgarian great-grandparents."

Connie smiled. "But I will see real Thulgarians if you take me to Chicago while the royal family is here. Please! I've never wanted anything so much in my life." She was going to use the guilt tactic and say how there were so many things she couldn't do because of her "condition," but she decided to hold that in reserve.

Maybe her parents were thinking along those lines anyway. They looked at each other, then her mother said, "We'll see. It isn't until May. We'll see."

Connie knew what "we'll see" meant. A crack was open. She'd have to launch a steady campaign of persuasion, low-keyed enough not to drive them crazy but persistent enough so they didn't forget how important it was.

Though they learned about it later than Connie, the American media soon began picking up on the approaching royal visit. Thulgaria was hardly a major power, but the American people found it quaint and romantic, a staunchly independent little country holding out against centuries of European upheaval. And besides, it was a monarchy. For all their commitment to democracy, Americans loved kings and queens and all the trappings that went with them.

Connie cut out all the newspaper and magazine stories on the subject, and was in ecstasy when specials on Thulgaria began to be shown on TV.

Whenever Connie and Rudy were together, they tried to do what planning they could, but it was difficult. They knew where the Thulgarian delegation would be staying, and they had an outline of the itinerary, but arranging an actual meeting wasn't easy. Still they were determined to do so. After all these years, they simply had to meet each other in person.

For her part, Connie was considering sneaking away and taking a bus to Chicago during the royal visit. But it turned out she wouldn't have to. Her mother agreed they'd make a special outing of it, even skipping a couple half-days of school. Connie knew there were some of the usual parental motives behind this. She had overheard her mother telling her father that at least this interest was getting Connie out of her shy, introspective shell. They ought to encourage this sort of independence and assertiveness.

All right, Connie decided, encouraged to plan further. They'd drive up, stay in a cheaper hotel near the Thulgarians', then join the crowd waiting outside the posh hotel for a glimpse of the royal guests. What happened next, she realized, depended on a lot of luck.

Connie didn't have any really close friends at school, though some kids were friendly enough, and of course there was a special bond between all runners, whether they were members of the track team, or hangers on, like Connie. But she was so excited about the upcoming events, she couldn't help telling everybody about them.

Some people were interested, but most scoffed at the whole idea of being worked up about a little country no one had ever heard of. This provoked Connie to tell them more than they wanted to hear about Thulgaria. When some kids began making fun of a crown prince who had the same name as a reindeer, Connie decided to give up and keep her excitement to herself. The only person besides family to whom she said any more was her friend Linda who thought that the prince with the curly black hair was devastatingly cute.

Finally the time came. Connie couldn't be pried from the television news when it covered the royal visit to Washington, D.C. Commentators gushed about the queen's wardrobe and the regal-looking king who despite his short stature was very dashing with his clipped gray beard and white uniform bedecked with sashes, medals, and gold braid.

They made less mention of quiet, rather shy Crown Prince Rudolph, except to say that his English seemed the best of the lot. But the reporters were captivated by the pudgy bouncy princess. Connie knew she was only here after hours of tantrums over being left out, and many solemn vows to be good as gold the entire trip. So far, she seemed to be doing pretty well, and Connie smiled fondly whenever she saw her cherubic face on TV. After all, Princess Charlotte was the closest she had to a little sister, and Connie had the advantage of not having to put up with her all the time.

When the royal family departed by plane for Chicago, Connie and her mother left by car for the same destination. They'd no sooner checked into their hotel than Connie was dragging her mother out the door and up the street toward the fancy VIP hotel. There was already a small crowd milling around the entrance hoping for a glimpse of royalty. The police had erected wooden sawhorses to keep people back from the strip of red carpet under the hotel's marquee.

After a few minutes, Connie cautiously slipped away from her mother and inched between people to the front of the crowd. Flushed with excitement, she leaned on the wooden barrier and waited. Soon a mur-

mur fluttered through the crowd and sirens were heard in the distance. They were coming!

Connie stood on tiptoe to catch sight of the motorcycle escort and the long black limousine with two Thulgarian flags flapping from its grille. The car pulled to the curb and a uniformed hotel doorman walked pompously down the red carpet and opened the car door.

A short dapper man with a trim gray beard stepped out, and the crowd clapped and cheered. He waved rather shyly at them, then reached inside and helped his wife alight. Next a little blond girl bounded out, followed more sedately by an older boy with curly black hair.

As the royal party walked toward the hotel door, acknowledging the cheering around them, the boy kept shyly scanning the crowd. He was almost up to her when Connie leaned over the barricade and shouted, "Rudy!"

Their eyes locked. Smiling, he swiftly stepped forward and grabbed her hands. As they leaned close together, Connie whispered, "Meet you in the Xanadu Room restaurant as soon as they think we're asleep."

Rudy squeezed her hand, then swept after the others. Charlotte looked at her brother quizzically. "You know her?"

"How could I? It's just an American custom, 'pressing the flesh.' American leaders always try to shake any hand in reach."

Charlotte nodded, then trotted to the barricades and began shaking hands with the delighted spectators until her brother grabbed her shoulders and piloted her toward the grand brass door. But before the doorman closed it after him, the crown prince of Thulgaria looked back into the crowd and smiled broadly.

CHAPTER 5

That night Connie and her mother ate dinner at a Chinese restaurant. She knew the royal family was attending a banquet for city notables and the leaders of Chicago's Thulgarian-American community. Connie had thought about trying to sneak into that, maybe disguised as a waitress, but had decided this other plan was better.

After dinner, she and her mother did a little window-shopping, then returned to their hotel room. For a while they watched TV on a screen three times the size of the one at home. But Connie, frantic to have her mother get to sleep, complained that she was tired. The TV was turned off, and mother and daughter got into their beds, each, Connie decided, large enough to hold a regiment of Thulgarian soldiers.

It seemed forever before her mother's breathing slipped into a soft regular pattern. Then, cringing against the slightest noise, Connie slid out of bed and tiptoed to the bathroom. She pulled on the skirt and blouse she'd hidden under the towels, then, checking that her mother was still asleep, she crept to the door of their room and slipped out. Patting a pocket to be sure she had the key, she pulled the door closed with a soft click. She flitted ghostlike down the hall, punched the elevator button, and waited in a billowy cloud of excitement.

Once outside the hotel door, Connie looked along the now largely deserted sidewalk. She'd read once that to avoid muggers, if you have to be out in a city at night, you should walk with determination. She had plenty of that. She started off at a steady determined stride.

At the gleaming brass door of the posh hotel, however, she slowed. The doorman looked her over, and she was glad she'd decided to wear a skirt instead of jeans. Then trying to look as if she belonged in this sort of place, she walked boldly past him and found herself in the magnificent lobby of the hotel.

The wine-colored carpet was as thick as a well-tended lawn, and the walls glowed with polished wood, velvety wallpaper, and crystal light fixtures. The vast room was at least three stories high, with painted cherubs flying around on the distant, pale blue ceiling. At the far end, a marble staircase cascaded down like an orderly white waterfall. She figured Rudy would feel

51

right at home here. She also figured that if she hadn't had plenty of mental experiences with real royal palaces, she'd turn around and run right out.

Concentrating on not being intimidated, she looked around for the Xanadu Room restaurant. She'd read brochures about this hotel as soon as she'd learned where the Thulgarians would be staying. The Xanadu Room was supposed to be somewhere off the lobby. It sounded posh and expensive, but it also was supposed to be open until three o'clock every morning. It was only a little after midnight now.

Finally she found the gold-and-mahogany sign almost hidden behind a jungle of potted palms. The head waiter, standing at the door, gave her a look that turned her skirt and blouse into Cinderella's rags.

She cleared her throat, trying for something more than a mouselike squeak. "I'm meeting someone here. Is there a boy my age already waiting?"

"I'm afraid not, miss."

"Well then, show me to a table for two. A secluded table."

Connie was surprised when the waiter did just that. She'd never been to a restaurant like this before, but that's the way people talked in them in the movies.

Sitting down, she stared with some awe at the table before her. The silverware gleamed like mirrors, and the rosebud in its vase, and the little candle lamp all matched the subdued colors of the wallpaper, tablecloth, and napkins. The napkin was the most intimidating thing of all. It fanned out at her place like the spread tail of a peacock. She was afraid to disturb it. Instead she cautiously sipped at a goblet of ice water and looked at the leather-bound menu the waiter brought her. In the background someone was playing a harp—not a recording, but a real harp.

She blanched at the prices, glad she'd dumped most of her saved up allowance into her purse. Why, she wondered, did a fancy setting make food cost ten times as much?

"Hello, Connie."

She looked up. There he was, the boy she'd known since the day she'd been born, but had only met today.

"Rudy! Come on, sit down. Did you have trouble slipping away?"

He sat opposite her. "Yes. Tot and I are sharing a suite. She's got a separate room, but she kept barging into mine and babbling about all the stuff we've been seeing. Finally I told her that if she didn't shut up and get some sleep, she'd be left behind with the Thulgarian Americans and wouldn't get to see Disneyland."

"And?"

"That knocked her out like a hammer."

A waiter eased up to them. "Would you young people like to order now?"

Connie said they needed more time to look at the menu, then they both fell to studying it in earnest.

"What I want," Rudy said, "is ice cream, gobs of

53

it. Whenever I'm with you and you eat American ice cream, I get frantic to taste it. All we usually have in Thulgaria is chocolate, vanilla, or strawberry."

They decided on a Butter Brickle Caramel Crusher and a Chocolate Cherry Crunch Supreme. Then they really started talking. Connie had wondered if, when they actually met each other, they'd be tongue-tied. She needn't have worried. It was as if a flood had been loosed.

Between spoonfuls of their enormous dishes of ice cream, they talked about Rudy's trip, Connie's cat who was about to have kittens, and all the little things they'd always wanted to know about each other and somehow had missed. What was the part they most enjoyed doing in a jigsaw puzzle? Did they eat the frosting or the cake first? What was their favorite color and their favorite time of day? Always the answers were identical.

Then they talked about past and possible future attempts to regulate their mental visits. Would it ever be possible to bring them on or decline them at will? Could they learn to communicate without passing out? Could they ever manage to exchange thoughts as well as sights and sounds?

Finally Connie asked, "Do you think we're the only people in the world who have this thing?"

Rudy shook his head. "I doubt it. Some scientists take ESP pretty seriously. I bet lots of people have this sort of thing. But they probably don't talk about it, and if they go to doctors, they probably don't get any more explanation than we have."

"Yes. You know, that could explain a lot. Maybe some of those people in the past who were accused of witchcraft were just people like us talking to friends who weren't there and learning things they wouldn't have otherwise."

"And people 'speaking in tongues.' They could simply be talking in the language of the other person."

Connie nodded excitedly. "Joan of Arc's voices could have been someone she was linked to in China or someplace."

"Hmm, and those who had it may have really thought they were crazy. We're lucky we've had news-papers and TV. I mean, I grew up knowing there really were little midwestern American towns like the one I kept visiting.

"Yes," Connie nodded. "I remember the first time I actually saw a picture of you and your palace in a magazine. It was like being told my visits weren't just crazy imaginings. It was all real, no matter what anyone else might say."

Rudy frowned. "And I still don't want to give them a chance to say anything."

"Despite what your uncle Albrecht said?"

His mouth twitched with pain. "No. Even if we tell the truth, people will find some way to twist it.

They don't tell me a lot, but I sense there's some real political dissatisfaction in the parliament and the palace. And there are rumors, some of them about me and 'my health.' I know now I should have paid much closer attention to all this. I'll have to from now on. But there's more at stake than simply my chance at the throne. It's all tied up with wanting to end Thulgaria's neutrality. And that, I'm sure now, is very very wrong."

"Well, I'll do whatever you think best, Rudy. The most important thing to me is that you don't get cheated out of your right to be king, which you have to be before you can do anything with your political ideas. Don't get me wrong, I love your dad almost like my own, and I want him to be king as long as possible, but when the time comes for someone else to do it, that ought to be you."

Rudy looked thoughtful for a moment, then he chuckled. "Yes, I do want that, though at times I'm really not sure why. I don't like those long dull receptions any better than Tot does. Oh some of the hors d'oeuvres are pretty good, but I hate all those platters with slimy looking sliced fish."

"That's just because you've been Americanized from the cradle. When you become king, pizza or chips and dip can replace the sliced fish."

"And then I can make skateboarding the national sport!"

"And . . ."

They felt someone standing over them. Looking up at the same time, they both said, "Wolfie!"

The tutor blinked in confusion at Connie, then focused on Rudy. "Your Highness, I believe you should be in bed resting up for tomorrow's activities."

"Probably. But how did you know I wasn't?"

Wolfie replied in German, assuming the American girl would not understand. "Charlotte told me. She came to my room, said you were missing, and that she thought you'd made a date with a teenage American blond."

Rudy snorted. "What a nosy pest that kid is. But smart too, going to you instead of my parents. They might not understand that an important part of a trip to America is eating large ice cream concoctions with pretty American girls."

He turned to Connie and winked, switching into English so Wolfie wouldn't catch on that she'd understood the German. "I'm afraid I must depart. It has been a very pleasant evening, but before I go, please do finish telling me about that movie plot. We don't get many American movies in Thulgaria, and I may never learn how it came out unless you tell me."

For a moment Connie looked confused, then she remembered. Somehow with all their other concerns, she'd never told him how that movie had come out. "Oh yes. Well, the hero finally defeats the arch-dragon in a riddle contest, then they get into a battle that destroys half the mountain and traps the dragon forever in a cave at the bottom of a lake. The hero and shepherdess return to what's left of his original village and settle down, deciding that 'living an interesting life' is part curse and part blessing."

With a twitch of a smile, Rudy said, "sounds a little like a lesson from Thulgarian history." Standing up, he bowed to Connie. "May we meet again in times that are not *too* interesting."

The prince and his tutor left, and when Connie tried to pay the bill, she learned that Wolfie had charged it to the Thulgarian account.

She found her way back to her hotel in a haze of happiness and slipped into her room and bed without her mother stirring. Good thing, she thought sleepily, that she had a nosy little sister only part of the time.

In the morning, Connie was too happy to be tired. She was standing in front of the mirror, brushing her hair and thinking about Rudy when suddenly she felt very odd, both tingly and stretchy at once. Then she was profoundly dizzy, but there was clear reason for that. She was still awake, but she was seeing two places at once.

She could see everything in the room around her as she staggered to her bed, dropped down, and stared woozily at the large painting of flying ducks. At the same time she could see another, far more elegant hotel room with Princess Charlotte sitting on a plush rug playing with a set of Indian dolls.

Rudy had apparently been trying to tie his necktie, but now he sat dizzily in a chair, blinking as his vision and Connie's overlapped.

Connie's mother, coming out of the bathroom, stared at her daughter. "Are you having one of your spells, Connie?"

"No," Connie said slowly, still seeing both scenes like a double exposure. "Not one of the big ones, and not one of the little ones either. Something in between."

The view of Rudy's hotel room seemed to bob up and down as if he were nodding his head. "Yes," she heard him saying, "I was just thinking about you. Maybe this is happening because we're so close right now."

"What's happening because we're so close?" Charlotte asked, looking up from her dolls. "Uh-oh, Rudy, you look funny. Are you going to have to hurry and lie down?"

"I don't think so," he said carefully, standing up. "I can even still walk, if I can just figure out which picture my feet are in."

"You're talking pretty funny too. Should I call Mama?"

"No. I'm just having an interesting time, that's all."

Now Connie nodded. "That's true enough."

"What's true enough?" her mother asked sharply.

Connie looked at her mother, trying to separate her thin worried face from Charlotte's plump childish one. "Oh, I was thinking of the saying about how interesting times are not always easy, but they're never dull."

Carefully Connie got up and finished packing.

After a few minutes, the double picture faded and disappeared, leaving both her and Rudy with pounding headaches.

When her mother felt certain Connie was staying conscious, they checked out of the hotel, loaded the bags in the car, and started the drive back home. After another day of official events and yet another banquet, Rudy and his family also left Chicago, taking a flight to Los Angeles.

They experienced no more strange double-sighted episodes, though two days later Connie had one of her regular spells and got in on several rides at Disneyland as well as being with Rudy while he consumed a triple-scoop American ice-cream cone. He also managed to be alone long enough to say he'd tried and failed to bring on her visit earlier when they were touring Universal Studios. Clearly, if distance had anything to do with changing things, it had to be a very short distance, as it had been in Chicago.

Finally the Thulgarian state visit to the United States ended, and the lives of both families got back to normal. Connie no longer watched the TV news as avidly and stopped trying to work the subject of Thulgaria into every conversation, though at school her sort of friend Linda was terribly impressed that she'd actually gotten to shake "that cute prince's" hand. Connie had also managed to collect quite a crop of Thulgaria-related pictures from recent newspapers and magazines, and she spent happy hours finding appropriate places for them on her walls and in her scrapbooks.

Once back home, Rudy returned to his regular lesson routine. One of the disadvantages, he decided, of having a tutor instead of going to school like Connie, was that there were no summer vacations. He could tell that Wolfie wanted to know what had happened in Chicago and how he'd managed to arrange a date with an American girl on such short notice. But his tutor respected his privacy too much to ask, and for that Rudy was grateful.

Life went on pretty much as it had before until one evening in July when Connie had another of her spells. There seemed nothing unusual about it at first. They'd gone to a barbecue at Aunt Sherry's house, and in the fading summer light the younger people were playing volleyball on the lawn. Connie suddenly excused herself and hurried inside to lie down. She made it to the living room couch, and for a couple of hours the family, quite used to this sort of thing, carried on its activities around her.

About ten o'clock, however, Connie suddenly sat

up screaming. She jumped to her feet and stumbled toward the kitchen, colliding with her mother and aunt who were hurrying out to see what was the matter.

Eyes wide with terror, she grabbed her mother and began shouting, "Call the police, call the army! The king must be told! I've been kidnapped!"

CHAPTER

6

As Connie had hurried from the volleyball game into the house she'd just had time to realize that with the time difference, it would be the middle of the night in Thulgaria. Great. She'd probably move into Rudy's mind when he was asleep. She'd done that before. Very dull.

Soon that's exactly where she was. Everything was dark and quiet. Rudy might have been having dreams, but the way this thing worked she couldn't tap into them any more than she could into his waking thoughts. She just hoped this visit wouldn't last too long. She'd rather be playing volleyball, even on a hot sticky midwestern evening. And there was still the watermelon too.

Suddenly, however, things changed. There were odd jarring noises. Rudy's eyes flew open. Shapes were moving around in the darkened room. Human shapes.

One bent down and whispered in a deep foreign-sounding voice, "Get up, get dressed, and don't make a sound. I've got a gun with a silencer aimed at your head. Do everything exactly as I say."

Confused, angry, and not a little afraid, Rudy got up and began pulling on the clothes thrust at him. The faces on the dark figures around him were blank, probably wearing some sort of masks. He could, however, see the dull gleam of what might be a gun.

Beside him, there was a strange scritching noise and hands were raised toward his face. He flinched, but couldn't avoid the strips of tape that were tightly wrapped around his head covering his mouth.

Someone pushed him toward the door of his room, and again the deep voice hissed in his ear. "No noise or you're dead."

He was hustled along the hall, then down a set of back stairs. On one landing, he thought he saw a sprawled body. A guard? He was hustled past. Once outside a dark green car was waiting, engine running quietly but with no headlights. A back door opened, he was thrust inside, and before he could even see which gate they were using, more tape was wrapped tightly across his eyes. Only after a few minutes of jolting along in the darkness, did Rudy realize he was not alone. Connie was with him. He had missed the telltale arrival dizziness while he was asleep. He appreciated her presence, though she was every bit as blind, and probably nearly as afraid as he.

The two big fellows riding on either side of him

were silent most of the time, and Rudy strained to listen to the sounds of the ride. He could pretty well tell when the car had left the city for the quieter countryside. There was no clue, however, as to which direction they were headed.

The trip seemed to go on forever, and after a while the roads became fairly twisty. Rudy was glad he didn't get carsick. With his mouth taped, that could be disasterous. More than ever he wished he could share thoughts, or at least emotions, with his visitor, but they were both trapped in isolation.

Then at last, he noticed a change in the sound of the road. Paving had given way to gravel. They seemed to drive uphill for a while then the car slowed to a stop. The door opened to fresh early morning air and a waft of bird song. He was dragged roughly outside. On cramped legs, he staggered in the direction he was pulled, his feet crunching on gravel.

He heard a heavy sounding door open, and was whisked inside some building. The ceiling felt far away and the air was cold and slightly musty. Someone was still pushing him forward over a hard stone floor. Suddenly something jammed against his toes and he fell forward bashing a knee and a shoulder on what felt like stone steps.

"Idiot!" the deep foreign voice said from nearby. "Take the tape off so he can see to climb the stairs. I'm not carrying Prince Charming up like a baby."

Someone grabbed the tape around his eyes and

started pulling. It hurt worse than all the bandages he'd ever pulled off of scabs. The tape that was yanked from around his mouth was almost as bad, but somehow he managed not to whimper.

"Up!" the man said behind him with an accompanying push in the back.

Rudy began to climb. Up and up the stone stairs spiraled, passing regularly spaced slots, narrow windows in what appeared to be thick stone walls. Out of the first he could see gray early morning light and a welter of leaves. Through the second came trees and sky, but the third gave a view over wooded hillsides down into what appeared to be a river valley. On the far side rose another hill, almost a mountain. Through the trees, a scattering of red roofs and several steeples could be seen, while above these, on the crest of the hill, a tall gangly metal tower jutted up like a skeletal giant. The sun, rising somewhere behind him, glinted off its silver struts.

"How much higher?" Rudy asked, turning around to look at the now unmasked man coming up behind him.

"Shut up and climb," came the growled reply.

Suddenly Rudy felt tingly. Connie was leaving him, but not before she too caught a glimpse of the man's face in the pale shaft of morning light. The eyes were blue, the cheekbones high, and the hair was cut short and flat like the bristles of a brush.

＊　　＊　　＊

When Connie finally calmed down and sorted out who and where she was, she was too upset to be embarrassed by her behavior. But she knew she had to act calm and collected or they wouldn't call the police, they'd call doctors with sedatives.

"Sorry," she stammered, as her mother and aunt fussed over her and several curious cousins stared at her from doorways. "That was really a lot worse than usual. But I'm fine now."

"Are you sure?" Aunt Sherry said, "You look a little pale."

"Oh yes. I'm just fine. A little tired though. Could . . . could I maybe sit down for a while and just listen to the radio?"

Soon Connie was sitting in a big comfortable chair in the study with a radio turned on beside her. Desperately she flipped through stations trying to find a news program. There were plenty of fairly ordinary things happening in the world but no reports of the crown prince of Thulgaria being kidnapped. Of course, maybe no one had found his empty bed yet.

That night at home, when she was supposed to be asleep in bed, she stayed up very late listening to her own radio. Still nothing.

What could have happened? she wondered. It wouldn't do any good for her to call the police or the Thulgarian embassy. Surely they knew Prince Rudolph was missing by now. But why was there nothing on the news? It was certainly a big enough story.

The next day there was still no news coming out of Thulgaria. Did the king and queen have some reason for not telling the press? Maybe they were negotiating with the kidnappers, and being quiet was part of the deal. But what would kidnappers ask for in order to release Rudy? And would the king and queen pay it? Maybe they couldn't, or maybe, like some countries, they didn't believe in ransoming hostages. What would happen then? Would the kidnappers kill Rudy?

At the thought, Connie felt cold. Could he be dead already? No! Surely she would know that. She may not know where he was, but she was certain he was alive.

But wait a minute, she wasn't totally in the dark about his location. She had seen a little, painfully little, but it was something. He was in some sort of old stone building set in wooded mountains. The sun rises in the east, so the valley she had seen had been to the west. Above the valley was a hill with a red-roofed village and topped by some sort of radio or electrical tower. All this didn't mean a lot to her, she admitted, but to someone more familiar with Thulgaria . . .

Suddenly she knew what she had to do.

CHAPTER 7

For the rest of the day, Connie tried to keep to her room. She was so tense and impatient she felt like exploding, but if her parents noticed they might think she was sick and suggest that the two of them should stay home instead of going to the party they had been invited to that evening. Connie needed them out, and she needed them out late.

In the late afternoon, Connie heard the shower running and smelled the waft of her mother's perfume sliding under the door. They were getting ready. She emerged from her room long enough to wish them a good time. Yes, they should stay out as late as they wanted. There was some good stuff on TV, and she could handle the frozen dinner just fine.

The moment their car eased down the driveway and disappeared up the street, Connie bolted for her room. Grabbing her *Complete Traveler's and Business-*

man's *Guide to Thulgaria*, she hurried back downstairs to the hall telephone. Plunking the guide down on the table, she turned to the page she had marked. There were two numbers given for the royal palace, one for tour information and the other, the one she'd underlined in red, for people calling on government business.

She glanced up at the hall clock, and though she knew what it would say, she could have screamed in frustration. No point in calling now. It was the middle of the night there, nobody would answer. She'd have to wait until past midnight here. Her parents had sure better stay out late.

The evening passed with excruciating slowness. She cooked her dinner and watched a string of shows on TV without really noticing any of them. But at long last, midnight came and she returned to the hall.

She placed a hand on the receiver, then stopped. This was going to cost a fortune. But her parents wouldn't know until they got the phone bill next month. Taking a deep quavery breath, she lifted the receiver and dialed for the operator, explaining, when the flat disinterested voice came on, that she wanted to make an overseas call. She gave the number she wanted, then listened to clicks and whines. Suddenly, and quite clearly, a phone was ringing. Her pulse beat loudly. She'd made a phone ring a quarter of the way around the globe.

"Good morning, Thulgarian Royal Palace," a woman's voice said in German. "May I help you?"

Nervously Connie switched into German. "Yes, I need to speak to Wolfgang Reichmann."

There was a silence, then the woman said, "This is not the proper number for that individual. Perhaps someone else can help you."

"No, please. I need to speak to Herr Reichmann."

"If you would state your business, perhaps I could switch you to the appropriate department."

"Please, this is urgent. This is a long distance call, an overseas call. I need to speak to Herr Reichmann personally."

"Just a minute, please." There was another click, a dead pause, then a different woman answered the phone.

"May I help you?"

Connie sizzled with impatience. "Yes. I am calling long distance on a very urgent matter. I need to speak to Wolfgang Reichmann immediately."

Silence stretched for seeming minutes. Then, "I am sorry, but Herr Reichmann is not able to come to the phone just now. May I take a message?"

Connie considered several swear words in German, then rejected them, trying to keep her voice level. "No. Please, this is a matter of life and death. I need to speak with Herr Reichmann right away. Tell him . . . tell him I know something he needs to know about his student."

71

"Just a moment, please." Another long pause, and a man's voice answered.

"Wolfgang Reichmann here. Who is this, please?"

"Wolfie! Thank God. This is Connie Hendricks. We weren't properly introduced, but I'm the girl who was having ice cream with Rudy in Chicago. Has he been returned yet?"

"What do you mean?"

"I mean Rudy. I know he was kidnapped yesterday morning, but I don't know if he's been found yet. Has he been returned?"

"What do you know about that?"

"I know where he is. No, no I don't really know that, but I have some clues as to where he's being held."

"And how have you learned this, may I ask?"

"He was able to get me a message of sorts. It's hard to explain on the phone. But I do have some clues that might help you find him."

"I agree, Fräulein, this is not something to discuss on this telephone. Please give me your address and telephone number, and I will be back in touch with you."

Connie told him what he asked, and the conversation closed. She'd no sooner put down the receiver than she heard the sound of her parents car in the driveway. She doused the light in the hall and charged upstairs to her room, leaving the door open a crack so she could hear the phone ring.

Hurriedly pulling on her nightgown, she lay stiffly in bed. Why hadn't Wolfie wanted to discuss Rudy on the phone? On *this* phone, he had said. Were the palace phones tapped? She hadn't really given it much thought, but the kidnappers might not be out just for money. It could be some sort of political plot. And that might mean some people in the palace could be involved.

What would Wolfie do now? Go down to the corner pay phone and call her again? She heard her parents shuffling about getting ready for bed, but still the phone didn't ring.

Hadn't he believed her? No, surely with Rudy kidnapped, Wolfie wouldn't pass up any lead. And he had met her in that Chicago restaurant, so he knew that much was true. She'd just have to wait for his move now. It didn't come and didn't come, and eventually she fell into a troubled sleep.

Her sleep was broken at last not by the telephone but by the doorbell chiming in the early morning stillness. Then came pounding on the front door.

Connie lay in her bed a moment, confused. Then she heard her father cursing and tromping heavily downstairs. She jumped up, pulled on a bathrobe, and ran out to look over the banister.

Scratching his head sleepily, her father opened

73

the door. Silhouetted against the gray light, two men in suits quickly stepped in and closed the door behind them.

One pulled out his wallet and showed his identification. "Good morning, are you Paul Hendricks?"

"Yes, but . . ."

"We're from the CIA. We have some questions to ask you and your family."

"CIA? Questions? Do you realize"—he glanced at the hall clock—"do you realize it's five-thirty in the morning?"

"Yes sir, we do. Is Connie Hendricks available?"

"Connie? You're nuts. Connie Hendricks is a fourteen-year-old kid. You've got the wrong place."

"It's all right, Dad," Connie said, starting down the stairs. "I think maybe it is me they want." She certainly hadn't expected this, and she had no intention of saying much to these two. But she had a pretty good idea what they'd come about.

"Connie," her mother said, appearing at the top of the stairs, "what is all this about?"

"It's probably about a phone call I made yesterday. But I didn't call these guys." She stared at them more boldly than she felt. "Who sent you, anyway?"

"We'll ask the questions, miss," one of them said with a humorless smile. "Could we perhaps all sit down?"

Mrs. Hendricks looked flustered, as if she was torn between wanting to play hostess and wanting to throw these intruders out. Finally, she ushered everyone into the living room.

"Now, Connie," her father asked when they were seated, "did you make some sort of prank call?"

"No! There was no prank. I have some very real information that I need to pass on, but not to them."

"Miss Hendricks . . ." one of the men began.

"No. I'm not going to tell *you* anything. I will only talk to Wolfgang Reichmann."

"Connie," her father said, "these men are from the CIA."

"How do you know that?"

"They showed me a card."

"So? Those things can be forged. I don't know who's working for whom in this whole thing. The only person I *know* I can trust is Wolfgang Reichmann. And I'm only talking to him."

The two men ignored the finality of that statement and started asking her questions. The questions sounded innocent enough, but Connie decided she'd better stick with complete silence. If there was some political plot going on in Thulgaria, how could she know what side the CIA might be on, even assuming these guys were from the CIA? Her only loyalty in this was to Prince Rudolph, and the only person who almost certainly shared that loyalty was his tutor.

Connie's father tried to get the men to say what this was all about, but they were as uncooperative as Connie. Finally Mrs. Hendricks gave up and went into the kitchen to fix some breakfast. Then they all, CIA men included, sat around the kitchen table and ate a very tense, silent meal.

Connie tried to remain cool and controlled. She wished she could tell her parents more but didn't dare in front of those agents. Her poor mom and dad looked so worried. Briefly she smiled inside. And they looked a good deal different from Rudy's parents. Where King Wilhelm was slender, quiet, and reserved, her own father was stout and boisterous. And their mothers were the reverse. Connie's mother was as thin and quiet as a shadow while Queen Catherine was plump and pushy. How odd, though. She loved all four of them as parents.

After the awkward meal, Mr. Hendricks pushed back his chair and said, "All right, this has all been very jolly, but if you two don't start telling us what Connie is accused of, I'm going to call the police and have you thrown out of here—no matter what it says on your little cards."

"Mr. Hendricks," the taller of the two said, "your daughter is not accused of anything. We do, however, have reason to believe that she may hold highly important information, and we are interested in receiving that information from her and learning how she came by it."

Her father looked at Connie questioningly. She stared at her clenched hands and said quietly, "And I am only interested in giving that information to Wolfgang Reichmann. So that's that."

"So who is this Wolfgang Reichmann character?" her father asked impatiently.

Connie remained silent and the shorter of the CIA men looked at his watch and said, "We should be learning that shortly."

Forty minutes later, the doorbell rang again. All three Hendrickses jumped up and ran to the door, but it was Mr. Hendricks who threw it open. A mousy-looking young man with a blond mustache and thick glasses stood on the doorstep.

"Wolfie!" Connie cried. It was all she could do to keep from hugging him.

With a confused frown he blinked at her while Mr. Hendricks said, "So, are you the mysterious Wolfgang Reichmann?"

"I don't know that I am particularly mysterious," he replied in German-accented English, "but that is my name, sir. May I come in?"

"Sure, the more the merrier. We love to start our mornings like this."

When they were all seated in the living room, Connie looked around the circle of expectant eyes and realized that a fourteen-year-long secret was about to end. There was no choice now. She took a deep breath.

"Wolfie, it's true what I told you on the phone.

I do know something about Rudy's kidnapping and where he's being held. But I won't say a thing with these two men here."

A smile twitched under the pale mustache. "Your discretion is admirable, Fräulein, though I do think your CIA can be trusted here. Nonetheless"—he turned to the two men—"I do believe you gentlemen may leave at this point. You may tell your superiors that I appreciate their prompt attention in this matter, and I am speaking on behalf of Their Majesties as well."

"All right, sir," the taller said, standing up. "You're the boss in this. We'll wait in the car outside in case you need us further."

When the two had left, Connie gave her parents an uneasy look, then finally launched into it.

"Wolfie, you know about Rudy's spells, his seizures."

The tutor stiffened slightly but nodded his head.

"Well, I have them too. I always have, ever since I was born—like Rudy. We've never told anyone what really happens during them. Well, actually we both tried when we were little, but people didn't understand, and we finally decided it was best just to pretend nothing happened when we were unconscious."

Connie was afraid to look at her parents, having just admitted that she'd lied to them all these years. So, eyes fixed on Wolfie, she hurried on.

"What really happens when one of us has a 'big spell' and passes out is that his or her mind sort of moves in alongside the other person's. It makes that person dizzy for a moment. You've seen it when Rudy gets those little attacks of dizziness."

Almost despite himself, Wolfie nodded.

"Well, when that happens, the person who is 'visiting' can see and hear everything the other person can. The person who appears to be unconscious is actually perfectly conscious someplace else."

Connie couldn't help seeing that Wolfie looked less than convinced. She still didn't dare look at her parents. "You don't believe me, do you?"

"Well . . . I . . . it is rather hard to accept."

Connie's father cleared his throat. "I'm afraid I have to agree with Mr. Reichmann on that, Connie."

"Yes but," Connie's mother began, "remember that EEG with the sort of ghost reading? The doctor said it was almost as if a nearly identical mind was being read at the same time."

"Yes, that's it!" Connie said emphatically. "It's some sort of ESP, I think, but I don't know how it works or why. I was afraid the doctor would find out what was happening and stop it. This contact has become very important to Rudy and me. We didn't want to be cured."

She jumped up and walked over to Wolfie. "But now I don't care. Rudy's too important. Remember how he asked you last fall if you agreed with Hamlet that 'there are more things in heaven and earth than are dreamt of in your philosophy'? You said you did, but that didn't mean you believed in pyramid power or UFOs. Well I don't know about those things either, but this, this mental thing, is real."

Wolfie was staring at her, opening and closing his mouth like a fish. "I—I did say that, I remember. You were . . . You mean you were with him then?"

"Yes. Just like I was with him day before yesterday when he was kidnapped. I didn't see all that much. It was still dark when they jerked him out of bed. They put tape over his mouth then hauled him down the back stairs. Was the guard I saw lying there all right?"

Dazed, Wolfie nodded his head.

"Good. Then they put Rudy in a car, a dark green one, I think, and taped up his eyes too. They drove through the city then out into the country, I could hear that much. The drive itself must have taken about two hours because Mom says I was out for about two and a half. The roads got winding, then we went up a gravel drive, and Rudy was taken into a building. They took the tape off him at the foot of some spiral stone stairs. That's when I saw what may be useful."

"And that was?"

"Well, the walls were a sort of reddish stone and very thick. There were narrow window slots on the round walls of the staircase. It was probably some sort of tower."

80

Wolfie was following the story very closely now. "Yes, and what did you see out of them?"

"Trees mostly. A lot of pines and also some others. But when we got up higher, I could tell that the building was on a hill or maybe a mountainside. There was a valley below, that I couldn't see into, but on the other side I could make out red tile roofs of a village with at least two steeples. And above them on top of the hill was some sort of electrical or radio tower. I know that was west of the building where Rudy was because the rising sun was reflected on it."

"And did you see any of the kidnappers?"

"Just one man with a really hard-looking face and a blond crew cut. He had a deep voice and some sort of foreign accent. But that's all I know because that's when I left."

"You say he had a foreign accent. You mean non-Thulgarian? But how could you recognize that?"

"Wolfie, I grew up with Rudy. I speak Thulgarian German as well as he does, just like he speaks American English as well as I do."

Wolfie looked at Connie's parents. Their stunned expressions were taking on a tinge of belief. "True," her father muttered, "she does speak perfect German."

The tutor sighed and turned back to Connie. "You say you left?"

"I woke up. We've tried, but we have no control over when we go or how long we stay in the other person's mind. But when I awoke this time, I guess I was pretty freaked out."

"Was that why you woke up screaming?" her mother asked. Then she looked at Wolfie. "I've never seen her so upset before. She's usually fine afterward, but this time all she wanted when she calmed down was to listen to the radio."

"That's because I was frantic to hear about the kidnapping on the news. But there's been no mention of it. Why?"

For a long moment Wolfie looked at her, then straightened up as if he'd made a decision. "Because we need to keep it secret. The kidnappers' conditions demand that."

He turned to Connie's parents. "Mr. and Mrs. Hendricks, I have a big request for you. There is no time now to debate the mechanics or the philosophy of what your daughter has been telling us. But I believe it is the truth. Suddenly there is just too much that fits for it to be otherwise. But because I do believe her, I need to ask you to let her return with me to Thulgaria."

Before they could answer, he turned to Connie and asked, "How often are you likely to have these spells?"

"Same as Rudy, it varies. Maybe one a week, sometimes less, sometimes more. I can't make one happen though, much as I'd like to now."

"No, I understand that, but if you do have one

and there's a chance of learning any more about where he is, then I'd like to be with you. Things at the palace are . . . very uncertain at present. You were right not to trust anyone. Even your call might have alerted someone it shouldn't have. But once you are in Their Majesties' care you should be all right. At the very least, you should be able to further identify that landscape."

"Now wait just a minute," Connie's father said. "I'm not about to let some stranger carry my daughter off to his comic opera country so that he can use her as some sort of living spy device."

"Daddy," Connie said, "I know this has all been awfully sudden. I often thought about how I'd tell you the truth, but I never expected it to be like this. But really, Wolfie isn't a stranger. I've known him since I was seven, since he started as Rudy's tutor. There's no one who's been kinder or more helpful to Rudy than Wolfie has. You've got to trust him."

Wolfie cast her a long grateful smile, then addressed her father. "Mr. Hendricks, I can understand what you are feeling, and believe me I have no intention of using your daughter like a machine. But you must understand that the future of the Thulgarian state may rest on her abilities. To say nothing of the life of a boy your daughter's age, a boy of whom I am very fond, as are his parents."

Connie's parents looked at each other, then her mother got up and hugged her. "Sweetheart, this is an awful lot to absorb in a very short time. We do love and trust you, I hope you know that. But are you sure you must go? It sounds more than just weird. It sounds awfully dangerous."

"Mom, I know it's hard to understand, but Rudy has been with you here as long as I have. Yes, I have to go help him, or try to. He's my best friend."

CHAPTER

8

The next few hours passed in a blur for Connie. She hastily dressed, threw some clothes into a small suit-case, and bid her parents a confused farewell. Wolfie was determined to catch the next flight to Thulgaria from the Chicago airport. A CIA man drove them there at breakneck speed.

Connie spent most of that drive sitting tensely beside Wolfie in the backseat, clutching her purse and staring at the rapidly passing landscape. She was glad her passport was still good from the time she'd gone with her parents to a conference in Glasgow. Wolfie had said that if it hadn't been, he probably could have arranged something through the Thulgarian embassy, but that would have taken time and alerted more peo-ple than necessary to what was going on. Something he didn't want to do.

She continued wondering about that until finally

she asked in German, "Wolfie, who do you think is behind this kidnapping? Is it just for money?"

He looked at her hesitantly a moment, then shrugged his shoulders. "One might think so. The Thulgarian royal family certainly has an attractive amount of wealth. But just before I left for here, we received the kidnappers' demands. It's political, I'm afraid. They want government policies on alliances and other matters to be changed, and they want the king to officially alter the line of succession."

"Oh," Connie said thoughtfully. "Then . . . then are Uncle Albrecht and his friends behind it?"

Wolfie looked at her sharply, then gave a grudging smile. "I keep forgetting we haven't any state secrets from you."

"Not if you don't have them from Rudy. Of course, I'm only there on and off, but I can usually piece together the missing bits. So you do think Albrecht is behind it? A few months ago he was trying to talk Mama, I mean the queen, into making Rudy not be heir any more."

"Rudy knew that?"

"Well, he overheard. Even the walls have ears, you know." Connie couldn't suppress a giggle.

"Hmm. You two *are* very much alike. All right, yes, *I* do think Duke Albrecht is partly behind this, but officially he's as surprised and upset as the rest of the royal family. One of the kidnappers' conditions is that we make neither the kidnapping nor the demands public. That way if it appears that the king has voluntarily agreed to these changes, the public will be more likely to accept them."

"But they're not going to agree to those demands are they?"

"Connie, you must know, Wilhelm and Catherine love their son very much, but they also love their country. Right now they are stalling to see if there aren't some other ways to go."

"Yes, I understand that, and they certainly won't let Rudy get hurt if they can help it. But they also mustn't let Albrecht get his way. Rudy wouldn't want that. He likes Albrecht, or he used to, but he thinks his ideas are all wrong."

"Yes, but the difficulty in trying to arrive at other solutions is not knowing who can be trusted. We know there are supporters of Albrecht's crazy ideas in parliament, in government offices, even in the palace itself. And they aren't all just power hungry. Some are very sincere and well-intentioned."

"Which is why you came here in person instead of talking to me on the phone."

"That and the fact that I didn't know who and what you were, and I didn't trust anyone else to find out." He smiled sheepishly. "Not that I was the least bit prepared for the truth when I did find it."

They made it to the airport and onto the big jet just minutes before it took off. This was Connie's first flight beside the one to Glasgow, but she didn't follow everything with as much interest as she might have. Worry got in the way.

Wolfie didn't want to talk about the kidnapping where they might be overheard. Still, shielded by the thick seats of the first-class cabin, they did talk about some of the experiences she and Rudy had shared. In the face of all the trivial day-to-day things that she knew, Wolfie's last traces of doubt obviously vanished.

After a time, though, conversation dwindled, and when the view below changed from toy landscape to distant gray ocean, Connie lost interest in her thick little window. The thrumming engines and the tinny distant-sounding voices lulled her into a series of naps interrupted by the arrival of plastic trays of almost delicious food.

Finally the trip became downright boring. Out of desperation she began looking through a gift catalogue from the seat pocket in front of her. Most was pretty useless looking stuff, though a thirteen-hundred-dollar china figurine looked nice. Suddenly she clutched the pages and sagged dizzily in her seat.

In alarm, Wolfie looked up from his own magazine. "Are you all right?"

"Yes," she said excitedly when her vision had cleared, "but Rudy is with me."

Wolfie looked flustered, "Can he—can he talk to me?"

"No, no, it doesn't work like that, but you can talk to him."

"How?"

"By just talking to me. He can see and hear everything I can, but we can't communicate back and forth, not immediately. You can tell him things, or if you ask a question he can answer it next time I'm with him."

"And when will that be?"

"Wolfie, I keep telling you, I don't know. If I could control this, I'd be with him right now, trying to figure out where he is."

"Yes. All right." He cleared his throat and looking awkwardly at Connie said, "Rudy, this is Wolfie."

"He knows that," Connie interrupted. "Really, he can see whatever I can."

"Oh yes. Well then, Rudy. Your friend Connie here is a very resourceful person. She telephoned me at the palace with just enough information to drag me over to America where she managed to convince me of this craziness. You know, I always thought there was more to those spells of yours than you let on, though I didn't expect this. Anyway, we're on our way back to Thulgaria and should be landing in Durstadt in about an hour and a half. With the time difference, that should make it very early morning. I guess what we need to know is where you are being held. I realize you can't tell us anything now, but when you, eh, get the chance, please try to pass on as much information as possible. Your mama and papa want you home safe and sound—and soon. And I must say, so do I. You're missing quite a few lessons, you know."

Wolfie laughed awkwardly, then said, "So what do I do now? Say 'over and out'?"

Connie shook her head. "I'm not a radio. He'll just be with us for a while. A long plane trip's not the most exciting experience to share, but it might be his most interesting choice at the moment. Why don't you ask that stewardess if she's got any science-fiction magazines. At least I can read something he'd like."

Wolfie shook his head. "An interesting concept. Reading for two."

When their flight took them back over land, Connie's interest in the window renewed. She found it hard to believe that those stretches of green and brown, cut by glittering rivers, were really the European countries she'd always heard about. It didn't look much different than flying over the United States. She figured the higher up you got, the more meaningless the boundaries people drew become.

Once they'd landed in Durstadt, the Thulgarian capital, and entered the airport, things started looking more foreign. But Connie realized with a thrill almost like homecoming that it didn't look unfamiliar to her, just non-American.

They quickly passed through customs and collected their luggage. Then before leaving the terminal,

Wolfie stopped in at the men's room. Connie, having visited the bouncing little bathroom on the plane just before landing, waited on a bench. She could still feel Rudy with her and decided she'd speak to him again, but just then another traveler came up, plunked his bag down beside her on the bench, and asked if she'd watch it for a minute. He was a jolly-looking fellow with a big handlebar mustache, the kind organ-grinders are supposed to have. She said she would, then he too disappeared into the men's room.

People kept wandering by, and Connie decided that if she was going to get a message to Rudy, she'd better find some place more secluded. Getting up, she walked across the lobby to where a rack of tourist brochures screened a portion of wall. There she could talk to Rudy out loud and still keep an eye on the luggage in her charge.

"Rudy," she said in a low voice, "I just want you to know that help's on the way, but that we can really use any clues you can give us." She stopped and waved at Wolfie, who'd just emerged from the men's room. "We need to know where you are, of course, but also anything about who is holding you and what their plans are, because . . ."

Suddenly the air rippled with light and sound then burst apart. Connie staggered back into the brochure rack, sending it jangling to the floor. Wolfie, who'd been walking toward her, was thrown on his face. On hands and knees, he kept scrabbling forward as the lobby behind him reddened with flame. He staggered to his feet, reached for Connie, and for a moment they clung together looking back toward the bench. Or where the bench had been.

"Our luggage!" Connie cried.

"Yes, but not us, as I think was intended. How did they slip a bomb into our things?"

"The man with the mustache!" Connie looked wildly around but saw no sign of him. "He left a bag beside ours and asked if I'd watch it for him."

"Clever. But how did they? . . . Never mind, let's get out of here. We don't want any public attention."

"But our bags."

"Goners by now. Besides, I thought American teenagers lived in nothing but jeans and T-shirts."

Connie looked down at her outfit. "I guess some of us'll have to."

Wolfie was already pushing their way toward the main door, fighting a crowd of people drawn by the explosion. Some looked like police.

"That's the palace limousine over there," he said when they'd made it outside. "I phoned from Chicago to have them send it." He frowned, then pulled Connie back into the shadow of the doorway. "Which could, of course, be how they knew when and where to find us. Sorry, I'm rather new to this James Bond stuff." Deliberately he headed in the opposite direction. "Who knows what might be waiting in the limousine. Let's rent a car."

While Wolfie hurriedly filled out forms at the car rental desk, Connie felt a wave of dizziness and realized Rudy had left them. Well, at least he knew they were safe for the moment. Then she looked at her other companion. A raw scuff mark spread across one cheek.

"Were you hurt much in that explosion?" she whispered.

"Not really. But when I fell, my glasses got twisted all askew. Now the world looks wobbly."

As soon as he was given the keys, Wolfie hurried out to the lot, his head down and scrunched into his jacket collar. "What I wouldn't give for the traditional trench coat and low hat to hide in. I feel awfully conspicuous."

Connie looked around nervously. There could be assassins around every corner. "Why do you think they wanted to kill you?"

"Us."

"Huh?"

"They probably wanted to kill both of us. See what our friend Rudy has gotten us into?"

"But I'm—they don't . . ."

"If they picked up that first call of yours to the palace, they knew I flew to America to meet someone who'd managed to learn something about the kidnapping. They couldn't know how you got your information or how much you knew. But it'd be safest to dispose of us both. Ah, here's our car."

Quickly they climbed into the little blue box of a car, and Wolfie drove out the back way. The thought that there might be people trying to kill her somewhat lessened Connie's enjoyment of the ride. Still, this was Durstadt, the capital of Thulgaria, Rudy's hometown. And a lot of it was familiar. Eagerly she looked at the statues and fountains, the orderly parks and the colorfully painted houses, sagging toward each other across narrow streets. She realized that their steadily upward route must be taking them to the palace, which crowned the hill overlooking the River Dur.

"We're going to the king and queen?" she asked.

"I had planned to. But after our welcome at the airport, I think I'll stop first at army headquarters. General Herberhausen heads up military intelligence, and he ought to be told what we know so far about the prince's location."

"What do we know?"

"A two-hour drive into mountains would take someone south and east of Durstadt but not as far as the border. Unfortunately, that area has a lot of red-roofed villages, and a lot of transmission towers. But it's a start. Also we know he's being kept in an old sandstone building with at least three floors and one round tower. Needless to say that area is also riddled with old castles and châteaux, some privately owned and some government property. Albrecht, if he is involved, could have access to a number of them. It's better than nothing, anyway."

Soon Connie recognized the distant walls of the palace. To their immediate left loomed another wall, high and windowless. Wolfie drove slowly along it until he came to a gate where he turned in, stopping at a guardhouse.

He leaned out of the car, showed some papers to the guard, and said, "I need to speak with General Herberhausen immediately."

"Just a minute, sir." The guard picked up a telephone. "Are you expected?"

"No, but I think the general will see me."

The young soldier spoke in a low voice into the receiver. After a minute he turned back to Wolfie. "You may proceed, sir. Drive across the plaza to the door on the far right." He pressed a button, which raised the wooden arm that had been barring their way.

Connie sighed with relief as the barrier dropped down behind them. They were in, and creepy bomb-planters were out. Disturbing a cloud of pigeons, they drove across the plaza and pulled to the curb. There Wolfie hurried them up the stairs and through a set of bronze-studded wooden doors.

A young woman behind a desk smiled when Wolfie gave his name. "General Herberhausen is expecting you."

Through another set of doors and into an elegantly furnished office, they were met by a stocky uniformed man who strode from behind his desk and clapped hands on Wolfie's narrow shoulders. "Wolfgang, good to see you again. Tell me, have you some news?"

Wolfie, trying to look as if he didn't mind the general's friendly shake said, "Not news, exactly. But with the assistance of Fräulein Hendricks here, we have some information on where the prince is being held."

An eyebrow crawled upward on the general's forehead. "Ah. That is good, then. Here, do sit down and tell me all you know." He indicated two straight-backed chairs in front of his desk and returned to his own chair behind it.

"I am not at liberty to divulge our sources, but suffice it to say that the prince was able to deliver a brief message to Fräulein Hendricks containing some information on his location. The first thing is that . . ."

A buzzer sounded on the general's desk. Frowning, the man jabbed at the intercom. "Yes?"

A voice muttered on the other side. The general's mouth twitched. He looked up. "My apologies. Someone is here with whom I must speak briefly. I will be right back."

Walking from behind his desk, the general opened a side door. Connie watched as he entered a larger, map-lined room in which a man stood, obviously waiting to see him. The door closed.

As soon as it did, Connie turned startled eyes on her companion. "Wolfie, we've got to leave here now!"

"Huh? No, we need to tell . . ."

"No, we don't! That man he had to talk to is the man who left the bomb at the airport."

"What? Are you sure?"

"I'd recognize that mustache anywhere."

"Then . . . then General Herberhausen must be . . . You're right. Let's get out of here!"

CHAPTER

9

In seconds Wolfie was out of his chair and sweeping Connie to the office door. He opened it, stepped into the lobby, and turned back to the now empty room. "Good bye, General," he said firmly. "Thank you for your time."

He closed the door, smiled at the receptionist, and with Connie close behind, strode to the outer door, exited, and trotted briskly down the steps to the car.

Once they were inside it, he started the engine and shot in a quick U-turn toward the gate. As they neared it, they could see the young guard talking on his telephone. Abruptly, he hung up the receiver, stepped from the booth, and holding up an arm called out, "Halt!"

Wolfie jammed his foot on the accelerator. Connie was thrown back into the seat as the car rocketed toward the gateway, smashed through the wooden barrier, and catapulted out into the street. The squeal of their tires didn't hide the single gunshot that twanged through the air after them.

From where she sat, slumped low in the seat, Connie saw that after starting down the way they'd come, they abruptly turned into what became a maze of twisting intersecting streets. Soon the sound of sirens rose behind them, but by then they seemed to have taken enough turns to lose an army of followers. Not, Connie noticed, that Wolfie was driving any slower because of that. Still, she realized, the regular traffic in Durstadt was frenzied enough to keep their speed, and wild weaving, from standing out. It wasn't until they'd left the city for the countryside that Wolfie slowed to anywhere near the speed limit.

When he did, he looked over at Connie and smiled shakily. "Just like in the movies, wasn't it? And I didn't even have a stunt driver." He shook his head. "Bet if I thought about what I was doing, I could never repeat that."

"Well, if you try, just let me out on the corner." She laughed weakly. "No, really, I was impressed. But where to now?"

"South toward the prince, I think. If Herberhausen is on their side, there's no telling whom we can trust. And now they're sure that we do know something. Even if I headed back to the king and queen, I'd probably be shot in a hallway before I could reach them."

Connie nodded, feeling more scared than she ever had in her life. "But, Wolfie, the two of us aren't exactly a SWAT team. Even if we can find out where Rudy is being held, we can't break him out on our own."

"No, but if we can pinpoint where he is, and reduce our information to one sentence, we can probably get that through to the king. And His Majesty is far more aware of palace politics than is his son's miserable tutor. He'll know who's loyal enough to send on a rescue mission or whatever."

Connie sighed and leaned back in the seat. Wolfie might not know a lot about palace politics, but he sure knew more than she did, or than Rudy for that matter. But if he wanted to live to become king, she decided, it was a hobby Rudy had better take up.

Forget the danger, Connie told herself in order to stop her shivering. Pretend you're on a tour bus. Look at the picturesque countryside.

And it was pretty. Under their tiled or shingled roofs, the neat white houses had colorfully painted shutters and window boxes filled with flowers. Some of the countryside was patched with fields but more was taken up by smooth rolling pastures where glossy brown cows grazed contentedly. The occasional villages were clustered around town squares with fountains or stone crosses at their centers. Then the road began to climb and groves of broad-leaved trees gave way to a dark blanket of pine and firs.

Connie had dropped into a half sleep when Wolfie

said, "I'm going to stop up ahead at the village of Kleindorf. For one thing, I'm practically starving, and for another, we need some tourist books for you to look at to see if you can recognize your view. Kleindorf is the jumping off place for tourists in the mountain district, so there should be plenty of guides and maps."

The village proved to be much like the others they had passed through only a little larger and busier. They parked on the edge of the town square. Along one side of the open plaza rose a red stone church with two towers that didn't match. Across from it stood a large half timbered building that Wolfie said was a sort of city hall. Along the other two sides of the square stretched a jumble of shops and restaurants.

Wolfie headed to one of the latter and bought them two little cardboard dishes holding sizzling brat-wurst tucked in a nest of thin french-fried potatoes. Balancing these, two soft drinks, and a wad of napkins, they headed to a bench on the square. Soon a collection of pigeons settled hopefully around them, but these were scattered when a little boy toddled into their midst squealing and flapping his arms.

Connie hadn't realized how hungry she was until she started eating. The sausage squirted hot juices down her chin, which she dabbed at absently. She felt she could have eaten ten of the things but wasn't sure her American health-food-trained stomach could handle quite that much grease.

"A slight improvement," Wolfie said when he'd

finished and tossed his cardboard tray into a trash can. "There're some touristy looking shops along the far side of the square. Let's give them a try."

The raised plaza that filled most of the square was paved with cobbles and thronging with pigeons, mothers with children, and lounging old men. Most of the children were clustered around the fountain in the center, sailing toy boats or dabbling feet. On a pedestal in the middle of the stone basin stood a bronze young woman surrounded by bronze geese. Water pouring steadily from a jar in her arms splashed over the geese and into the pool.

Connie had stopped to look at the bronze girl and her lifelike tumble of curls when she realized Wolfie was already starting to cross the street. She hurried to catch up and was just stepping off the curb when a car abruptly shot from a parking place and squealed down the road toward them. Before a cry could rise from her throat, it had hit Wolfie. He sprawled to the pavement. Without slowing, the car sped out of sight.

In seconds, Connie and several bystanders were kneeling beside him. His metal-framed glasses were smashed, blood was beading on the side of his face, and one arm looked oddly twisted. He was not unconscious, however.

"Connie," he gasped, blinking blearily at the crowd around him.

"I'm here." She leaned forward to hear his faint

voice over the babble of people calling for doctors, police, and ambulances.

With his good hand he grabbed hers.

"Playing very rough. Get away from here and hide or they'll get you next."

"But I can't . . ."

"Do it! You're our only link to Rudy. I'll try to get word to the king somehow. Hurry! They could be in this crowd right now."

Reluctantly Connie squeezed his hand and stood up. Then glancing nervously at the growing crowd, she slipped across the street. After half a block, desperate to get out of sight, she ducked into a tourist shop and went to the far aisle where she was screened by shelves and racks.

Without seeing a thing, she stared at a shelf of pottery steins, music boxes, and little wooden houses holding thermometers. All the while she strained to hear the sounds outside. "Deplorable," a voice said. "Hit and run." "Was he killed?" "No, but he could have been the way that madman was driving." The squeal of a siren interrupted, and Connie relaxed a little. Someone at least was going to take care of Wolf-ie. Once he was in a hospital maybe those thugs would leave him alone.

But what about her? In the course of a few hours, she'd been whisked out of her country, had her luggage blown up, been shot at, and now was left alone in a foreign village without any idea of where she was going.

Dejectedly she hooked a finger into a rack of postcards and sent it squeakily spinning. The selection of scenic vistas blurred before her. Suddenly her hand shot out and stopped the spinning rack. She stared at one postcard.

A dramatic rock outcrop rose over forested hills. At its base, the round towers of a stone castle stuck up from among the trees. In the background, on a distant hillside was a scattering of red roofs, and on the hilltop above that rose the faint outline of some sort of metal tower.

Trembling, Connie pulled the card from the rack. It was taken from farther back and at a slightly different angle, but perhaps if one were looking out of one of those round towers . . .

She flipped the card over and read, "Castle Himmelstein. Built in A.D. 1132 as a royal fortress. Remodeled extensively during the reign of Gustav III. Granted to Baron von Himmelstein in 1813. Private residence."

Holding the card as tightly as a talisman, Connie took it up to the counter. She clutched gratefully at her purse. At least she still had that along with her passport and the Thulgarian money Wolfie had given her at the airport.

"Excuse me," she said in German to the shopkeeper. "This certainly is an interesting looking castle. Is it anywhere around here?"

He looked at the card. "Castle Himmelstein. Yes, it's about a half hour's bus ride from here. You get off at the village of Himmelstein. I don't think the castle is open to the public, though there are a number of other castles in the area that are. We have some good guidebooks in the back if you are interested."

Connie said she was, then went to the back of the store to look them over. She selected the one with the biggest write-up on Himmelstein, and was about to return to the counter, when the bells over the shop's door jangled and a deep slightly foreign sounding voice said, "Shopkeeper, I am looking for a teenage American girl. Has any been in here lately?"

Connie held her breath. "American?" the shopkeeper replied. "No, haven't seen any all day except for an older couple this morning. Plenty of teenagers of course, what with school out, but no Americans."

She almost fainted with relief. So she really didn't have an American accent. Squinting through the book racks, all she could see was the top of the questioner's head, his crew-cut blond hair. A chill fluttered through her as he went out the door.

After a minute she ventured up to the counter, bought the book, and was told she could catch the bus in front of the candy store on the square. Then when the shopkeeper was busy with another customer, she slipped out the back door.

She found herself in a narrow alley, which after a ways opened onto a side street. She felt terribly conspicuous. The jeans were all right, since all Thulgarian teens seemed to be wearing them, but her SAVE THE CONDOR T-shirt was a little too American looking.

Staying to the side streets, she found a clothing store and bought an embroidered blouse like the ones she'd seen a lot of girls wearing. She slipped it over her T-shirt, then added one of the gaudy head scarves that seemed to be the local teen rage. Finally she braided her straight blond hair and fastened it with a plastic flower clasp for sale at the checkout counter. Glancing at a mirror she wasn't too pleased with the whole effect, but decided she at least looked a lot less American.

At last she worked up her courage to return to the square and look for the candy store bus stop. She studied the posted schedule, then, though nobody seemed to be looking people over, went inside the store and lingered by the magazines until the right bus rolled up about twenty minutes later. Quickly she got in, paid for one fare to Himmelstein, and sat down toward the back of the bus.

When the bus finally pulled out, she relaxed a little and tried to enjoy the scenery. It wasn't easy. She kept rerunning in her mind all the horrible things that had happened. She felt torn between screaming, crying, and yelling that she wanted her mommy. Better try to focus her attention on something else, she decided. Anything else.

In the seats behind her, several local teenagers were talking about an English rock group that even she had heard of. The girl and one of the boys thought they were terrific, but the other boy thought they stank and championed another group from Spain. Connie forced herself to listen.

The bus made two stops before the driver announced they were coming to Himmelstein. Connie jumped up, and behind her the three rock enthusiasts were also getting themselves together. As the bus pulled to a stop, she glanced out the window. Leaning against a lamppost, his eyes fixed on the bus, was a hard-faced man with a blond crew cut.

Instantly she felt sick. Should she stay on the bus? But who knew how far it would be to the next stop? As she hesitated, one of the boys from behind her began to push by.

Smiling radiantly at him, Connie clutched his arm and walked off the bus with him. "I really agree about those Spaniards," she said in her easy German, "but have you heard the Lizard Skins from Puerto Rico? Absolutely untouchable! Particularly Voodoo Varnie, their drummer. Sends chills up your spine."

"Eh . . . no," the bewildered boy replied. "They're that good, are they?"

The man with the crew cut gave them a brief glance then looked back at the bus door. Connie felt weak with relief but kept up the chatter until they were out of earshot. Then she let go of her escort's arm and smiled. "Come on over and listen to my tapes any time."

"Eh, yeah, sure, I'd like to." He gave his two other companions a pleading, questioning look.

Connie just waved at him and hurried around a corner, almost collapsing with laughter and not a little terror, when she was out of sight. Still, she was impressed. She'd never known she had it in her to do that sort of thing. Not exactly the shy introvert her mother had worried about.

Everything, however, was not going her way. For example, how had Crew Cut known to meet that bus? Had someone spotted her when she boarded it? No, they were probably just checking all ways into town looking for an American girl. They must think that she and Wolfie had known just where to go all along and figured that if either of them slipped through, they'd head here. She'd have to be very careful.

So, where to now? What she really wanted was to find a bed and go to sleep for about forty-eight hours. That transatlantic flight had completely messed up her internal clock. But there was no time.

She pulled the guidebook from her purse and flipped to the section on Himmelstein. There was a map of the village with dotted lines showing the main walking trails radiating from it. One was marked "To Castle Himmelstein: 6 kilometers." She set out in search of it.

It took a while to find where the line on the map translated to a real path on the ground, a search complicated by the fact that she had to keep looking for people who might be looking for her. But at last she found a signpost marking where the trailhead ran between a modest little stone church and the wall surrounding an old sleepy-looking cemetery.

Past the cemetery, the path led between two fields planted with neat rows of flowers. A florist supplier, she guessed, since surely even here people didn't eat flowers. Then the village and its suburbs came to an end, and the path dropped into dark woods.

Everywhere, tall evergreens rose like randomly spaced pillars. About twenty feet from the ground, they branched out into a roof of dark crisscrossed boughs. The late afternoon sun slanted between them like shafts of light through church windows. Here and there it lit clumps of ferns and wildflowers, but mostly the forest lay in deep shadow. The air smelled of moldy earth, its silence broken in spots by the ripple of bird song or the scolding chatter of a squirrel.

Tired as she was, Connie looked about with delight. Rudy had taken her into places like this, and always she had felt herself transported to pages of a fairy-tale book. She could easily imagine the Wolf waiting for Red Riding Hood around that big tree, or the gingerbread house appearing in the next clearing. There were even red-and-white-spotted mushrooms, though it seemed that the large orange slugs adorning some bushes were details artists had chosen to leave out.

Occasionally, she met people on the path and was regularly nodded to and wished a good day. But as the sun dropped lower, fewer people seemed to be about, and the sounds of forest animals increased. She wished she hadn't thought about wolves.

Still, when she forced herself to think about it, she knew that wild animals were probably the least of her problems. Here she was, totally exhausted, blundering along darkening forest paths, and not even certain if she was headed for the right goal. Discouraged, she stepped off the trail and sat amid a tangle of tree roots, which clutched at a mossy bank.

If Himmelstein wasn't the right place, she thought wearily, Rudy could be miles and miles away. Still, if it was right, then he'd be quite nearby. She recalled their years of failed experiments, and then what had happened to them that morning in Chicago.

Closing her eyes, she thought about Rudy, about his sharp-featured face and curly black hair, about his loneliness and uncertainties, but also his determination to become a good king. She thought about how scared he must be right now, and how alone.

Only he wasn't alone. She could see that now. A young man, maybe a guard, was sitting across from him in a small stone-walled room. Through the sudden dizziness, Connie could see that room almost as clearly as the forest around her. But she hadn't passed out.

The room was sparsely furnished, and the guard was sitting in a straight-backed chair in front of a cold sooty fireplace with a pile of firewood stacked beside it.

Rudy had been reading a book, but from the way it sagged in his hands, it was clear that he was suddenly as dizzy and bleary as she was. The guard continued reading his magazine, and soon the scene settled down.

Cautiously, Rudy got up and walked to the room's single narrow window. The view was much the same as Connie had seen before, except higher up. It took in more of the village on the opposite side, and showed a few glints of a river running down the intervening valley. The sun was just slipping behind the skeletal transmission tower on the far hilltop.

There were two exits to the room; one, a heavy wooden door, closed and apparently locked; the second was an arched stone opening leading to another similar room. Slowly, Rudy moved toward it, though clearly he was having difficulty walking with two different views before him.

The other room had no further exits and was furnished with one chair and a narrow wooden bed. Rudy walked to the single window and leaned unsteadily on the sill, looking out. Here the rocky hill on whose side the castle was built could be seen rising over the battlements of the adjacent wing. It's crest was crowned with a bare rock outcrop, the one Connie had noticed on the postcard. Several figures appeared to be moving across it, probably holiday climbers. Connie felt a wave of relief.

"Castle Himmelstein isn't it?" she said to the forest.

Rudy made a **V** sign with his fingers but said nothing.

The sun's setting rays glowed in the thick dust that frosted the window. Rudy turned and looked into the other room. He was out of sight of the guard, if not out of earshot. Deliberately, he raised a finger and began writing in the dust. G-R-O-T-T-O. Below that he wrote G-A-R-G-O-Y-L-E. Then he drew a circle with a dot in it. From the circle he drew an arrow and was just beginning to write a word at the end of the arrow when the guard walked into the room.

"If you're trying to write Help on the window Highness, no one'll be close enough but birds."

"No," Rudy said calmly smudging out his message, "I was just playing in the dirt." Yawning, he turned and looked at the guard. "Not that I don't appreciate your company, Heinrich, but is it really necessary to have a guard in here with me all the time? Wouldn't it be just as good to have someone on the landing outside the door or in the little room with the lion tapestry at the foot of the spiral stairs? Or perhaps you should have guards ringing the base of this tower in case I figure out how to open these windows and scale the sheer stone walls. Too bad old Gustav III didn't put his gargoyles on this part of the castle. Then I could probably manage the climb."

Heinrich snorted. "Can't say I like being cooped up here either. But those are the orders: Don't leave the prince alone. They don't want you to hurt yourself." His smile wasn't altogether friendly.

"I don't hurt myself, you know," Rudy said patiently. "If I'm going to pass out, I have plenty of warning. If anyone told you differently, he's lying to help excuse his usurpation."

"Another thing we're not to do," the guard said dryly, "is discuss politics or our plans with the prince."

By this time, Connie was getting used to this double vision enough to try walking. Standing up, she looked carefully down at the root-rippled earth then stepped back to the path. Step by step she continued along it, still seeing the tower room through the gloom of forest.

With greater ease, Rudy walked back to his chair. Suddenly he cried, "No!" To cover his blunder, he slapped at an imaginary mosquito.

Alone in the woods, Connie yelled the same. The dizziness passed as the second picture faded. Around her were nothing but trees and the sounds of a forest awakening to evening.

She felt as limp as a wet washcloth, and her head ached terribly. Maybe by concentrating, it was possible to bring on these strange spells of double vision, at least when the two of them were fairly close to each other. But she doubted if she'd be up to it again for a while. She felt far worse than she had in Chicago. But there they had only been a couple of blocks apart. Here it was closer to a couple of miles.

Still, though this episode had been all too short, she had learned some useful things. The identity of the castle was confirmed, but Rudy had managed to convey other information as well. For one thing, he always had a guard with him inside the room. That room was reached by spiral stairs with a landing on top and a little room with a lion tapestry at the bottom. There was no point in trying to get in or out of the windows because they didn't open and the walls outside were too sheer.

Then there was the thing about "grotto" and "gargoyle," and the circle with the dot. She didn't get that at all and wished he'd had a chance to finish his writing. Still, once she got a look at the castle, maybe she'd figure out what he meant.

She'd been fighting her headache and thinking all this over while slowly walking down the path. When she tripped over a root, she realized how dark it was becoming. Dusk had spread through the forest like mist. The few scraps of sky that silhouetted the treetops had become a deep distant blue. If she went on much longer, she was sure to get lost. Suddenly Connie realized this meant spending the night in the forest.

The idea did not appeal. Maybe she could find a cave or a snug thicket, but she kept thinking about wolves. Of course, that was just a fairy-tale holdover. There probably hadn't been wolves in these woods for centuries. Still . . .

The path had dropped into a narrow ravine. It looked as if, up ahead, it swung back against the base of the ridge that she had been angling down. Maybe she'd have better luck there finding a cave or rock overhang.

She followed the path around a large tree trunk and screamed. Ahead was a pair of large yellow eyes. Below them, a tongue lolled between sharp white teeth. Above the eyes rose dark pointed ears.

CHAPTER 10

"Young lady, you really mustn't scream at Heidi. It startles her."

Still trembling, Connie looked at the source of the voice: a portly old man wearing a cocky short-brimmed hat. A smile peeped out under his drooping gray mustache. In one hand he held a walking stick studded with little silver badges, in the other he held the leash of the biggest dog Connie had ever seen. It was the size of a pony.

"I'm s-sorry," she stammered in German. "But Heidi wasn't the only one who was startled."

The man chuckled and patted the dog's impressive shoulders. "True, one does not always meet a dog eye to eye like that. What did you think she was, a malevolent forest spirit?"

Connie looked down. "Actually I was thinking of wolves."

"No, no, great danes are much taller than wolves, friendlier too." He laughed again. "But which way are you going, Fraulein? Heidi and I would be happy to accompany you and frighten away all the real wolves."

Looking at the chubby old dog fancier, Connie decided that he was not very likely to be part of any palace conspiracy. "Well, I was heading for Castle Himmelstein before it got dark. Now I guess I'll have to camp in the woods somewhere and visit it in the morning."

The old man had turned his dog so that they were now accompanying Connie along the path. "Himmelstein is a fine-looking castle, certainly, but you will have to be content with just looking at it from the road. Baron von Himmelstein lives there, and it's not open to the public. There are some other very fine castles in the vicinity, though, if your heart is set on castle viewing."

"Yes, but I'm particularly interested in Himmelstein." Connie rummaged for an explanation that wouldn't peg her as an American but also wouldn't make her companion assume she knew things she did not.

"Eh . . . you see, my ancestors were Thulgarians who emigrated to . . . to Australia several generations back. Their name was Himmelstein, and I always had a fancy to come here and see the castle by that name. I'm in Durstadt on a student exchange and thought I'd run down here and see it."

"Australian? My, you certainly speak excellent German. I hardly detected any accent at all."

"Well, you see," she invented, "my grandparents still speak German at home, and I've spent a lot of time with them."

"Well then, my dear"—the old man swept off his hat and bent over in a crisp, slightly comical bow— "on behalf of the people of Himmelstein, let me welcome you home." Heidi joined in with an enthusiastic bark that sent a couple of roosting birds fluttering out of darkened bushes.

Trying to feel like an actress instead of a cheat, Connie bowed back. "On behalf of all wandering Thulgarians, I thank you."

"You realize, however," her companion said as they continued down the path, "that you really mustn't sleep out in the woods. Not that wolves are much of a bother these days, but a damp bed full of rocks and stickers won't leave you very refreshed for morning excursions. You must come and spend the night with Frau Müller and myself. Our grandson Otto is staying with us for a while, but we still have plenty of room."

Connie felt she ought to protest, but she was hungry and absolutely wrung out. The thought of sleeping in those gloomy woods definitely did not appeal. "That is a very kind invitation . . . Herr Müller?" He nodded, acknowledging his name. "And I think I would like to accept it. Do you live near here?"

He pointed with his walking stick up the slope. "Just past the edge of the village. Every evening Heidi and I take our constitutional down here. This week little Otto's been accompanying us, but tonight he wanted to stay home and finish his model."

Gratefully, Connie followed her host along a neat log-bordered path that zigzagged up the slope. Recalling the map in the guide book, she realized she must be nearing the spur of the ridge-top village that stuck out to the south. Rising on the other side of this ravine would be the hill crowned by the castle and the rock outcrop, and beyond that there'd be another bigger valley, the slope on its far side holding the village and tower she'd seen in the postcard. At least she was closer to the castle now, though she seemed to have wandered around some in the woods.

The Müllers' home, when they reached it, was warm and cozy. Frau Müller was even plumper than her husband, and almost immediately began serving up a delicious-smelling meal of meat pie and cabbage. Nine-year-old Otto was delighted to have a real foreigner in the house, and after showing off his spaceship model, heaped Connie with questions about Australia that kept her dodging for believable answers. She wished she had chosen some place she knew more about.

After a while Connie managed to turn the conversation away from herself and her "Australian background," to a discussion of Castle Himmelstein. Her

119

hosts related juicy details about their local pride and joy that the guidebook had left out. A crusader knight supposedly haunted the battlements; Gustav III had lavished enormous amounts of money on remodeling the building and grounds because it was where he had housed his favorite mistress; the first Baron von Himmelstein was deeded the castle by Frederick V because he'd exposed Napoleon's plot to conquer the kingdom. It was all very interesting stuff, but didn't shed much light on her problem.

Then as they were finishing their apple pastry dessert, Herr Müller said, "It really is a pity you can't get into the castle grounds for a closer look. It's quite a fantastic place with all the gardens and things. But there's a fence around the whole thing. There wasn't when I was a boy, mind you, not a very good one, anyway. And now they've cut us all off from the finest berry bushes in the whole kingdom. Otto and I can still find a few there, but it's not the way it used to be."

"Yes, Grandfather, but . . ."

The old man fixed the boy with a hushing stare. "Sadly, respectable people should respect fences, berries or not. Still, Otto, perhaps tomorrow you can take our guest down to the berry-picking spots beside the fence. The view's better there than from the road. Sorry I can't go myself, but I have work to do in the village."

By this time, though her headache had faded,

Connie was too tired to think about castles or fences. She fell asleep the moment she crawled into bed and in the morning woke up far later than she had intended. The tiny guest room, so cheery and neat in the mid-morning sun, made her feel again as if she'd fallen into a storybook. She dressed quickly, wishing that all her other clothes hadn't gone up in smoke.

Herr Müller had already left on his errand, but his wife was waiting with a huge breakfast of bread, jam, sausage, and cheese. Then, with Otto and Heidi as her guides, Connie set off. They went out the back way, through the bright flower garden, to where, beyond their gate, the well-used path wound down into the forest. It all looked a good deal cheerier than it had the night before.

As they walked along, Otto chattered as steadily as the birds around them, telling Connie about his school, his friends, his zillions of models at home. He liked spaceships best but also had some old-fashioned ocean ships and a few planes and cars. Then abruptly he stopped and grinned up at Connie.

"What do you think of that grandfather of mine?"

"He's a pretty sharp old guy."

"Yeah, he ought to go into military intelligence or something. He's pretty good at sending secret messages."

"What do you mean?" Connie asked sharply.

"That business about the berries. Grandpapa likes to pretend he's a real law-abiding citizen. He wouldn't think of directly suggesting you break any laws. That's why he wanted me to show you where to pick berries. He knows and I know that that's also the best place to get under the fence."

"Right." Connie nodded with an appreciative smile. "A pretty sharp old guy."

About ten minutes later, the wild forest ran up against a high wire fence. Beyond it, the trees had a much more tamed look.

"Castle grounds," Otto said. "We've got to follow along here until we get to the spot."

Otto had slipped Heidi free of her leash as soon as they were out of sight of his grandparents' house. She had kept up with them though, covering three times the distance by zigzagging back and forth through the woods. Now she came bounding back to them dripping wet.

Connie heard the stream before she saw it, since its banks were hidden behind a tangle of berry bushes. For a minute they forgot about forbidden entrances and concentrated on picking and eating luscious purple berries, sweet and warm in the sunlight.

Once their mouths and hands were thoroughly stained, Otto called Heidi back, clamped the leash on her collar and, pushing a way through the brambles, waded into the shallow stream. "Heidi really likes you, I can tell," he told Connie. "If I let her loose now, she might follow you through."

Connie gasped as the cold water seeped through the canvas of her shoes. Feet feeling heavy and clumsy, she walked up the stream, trying not to slip on the smooth mossy stones. Ahead of her, Heidi cavorted and splashed on the end of her long leash, occasionally stopping to shake, splattering her companions from head to foot. Connie decided she was very glad this behemoth of a dog liked her. Heidi would make a nasty enemy.

After a couple of twists in the stream, they came to a spot where the water gurgled under the wire fence. Here and there, the bottom strands actually cut into the flow, but way to the left there was a spot where a sandy bank was gouged out by high water. If one crouched down, there'd be plenty of room under the lowest barbs.

Otto bowed low. "Welcome, Fräulein, to Castle Himmelstein."

Connie's grin matched his, and she wished she had something to give him. No matter what happened inside, she wasn't likely to see either him or his grandparents again. Then she remembered the little airline wings which, to her horror, the stewardess had thought her young enough to have. After rummaging in her purse, she pinned them ceremoniously on Otto's shirt. "There. Maybe by the time you're old enough to be a real pilot, they'll be flying spaceships. Thanks for showing me where the best berries are."

123

Otto saluted, then he and Heidi splashed noisily back downstream. Connie squatted down and, feeling like a kindergartener pretending to be a duck, waddled under the fence. When she stood up on the other side, her former companions were already out of sight if not out of earshot. With considerably more stealth, Connie headed upstream.

As soon as the brambles began clearing back from the water's edge, she scrambled out onto the grassy bank. Her numbed feet oozed water at every step.

Looking up, Connie gazed around her. The grass here was less short and cropped than on a golf course, but it still looked far from wild. The trees, many varieties besides the dark evergreens of the forest, did not grow randomly but were clumped together in artistic little groups. From where she stood, it looked as if every grove housed a statue or bench or small columned temple. No doubt about it, mad king Gustav had been here all right.

And now so was she. But what was she going to do? Surely she had even less chance of being a hostage rescue team than she and Wolfie would have had. Yet what were her choices? Wolfie was off in a hospital somewhere, and she probably had no chance of slipping past the conspirators and reaching the king and queen by herself. She'd just have to go forward, try to find exactly where Rudy was being held, and hope that by being here there'd be some way she could help.

Looking again at the fantastic gardens, a thought came to her. Not only had the guidebook and the Müllers mentioned Gustav III, so had Rudy in her last brief visit with him. He'd also written "grotto" and "gargoyle." Why?

Both were apparently the sort of things mad Gustav liked, and maybe for some reason, Rudy wanted her to find some. That morning last fall, when Rudy had shown her the Grotto of Neptune, there had also been a lake. Maybe the circle and dot represented a lake with an island in it where there was a grotto or a gargoyle. It gave her something to look for anyway.

Of course, she could try to contact Rudy again, but she didn't want to risk feeling as wiped out now as yesterday's effort had made her. Maybe when she was closer, it wouldn't be so bad.

Keeping to the trees and shrubbery as much as possible, she began working her way uphill. Occasionally through distant trees, she caught a glimpse of red stone. Probably the castle. She just hoped there weren't a lot of guards and gardeners about.

She kept the stream in sight as her guide, figuring it might well flow from a lake, and after a while she realized she wasn't too likely to run into an army of gardeners. This place looked a lot more overgrown than the royal gardens at Durstadt. However, it had even more weird romantic buildings scattered about.

One appeared to be a miniature ruined cathedral,

probably built that way to look dramatic and moody. It might be fun to explore if she had more time, but as it was, she simply used it as a shield between herself and the view from the castle, which was becoming more visible through the trees. She'd just reached the shelter of the phony ruined walls when she felt a sharp pain in her ankle. She grabbed at it and felt a second jab on her wrist.

Snakes? Cold and sick with fear, she jumped back and stared into the weeds looking for telltale slithering. She saw nothing, but her ankle and wrist stung like crazy. Then she looked again at the weeds and would have laughed had she not been in so much pain.

Nettles. The plants didn't grow near her own home, but she remembered once when Rudy had blundered into a bunch and had jumped about as if he were on fire. Now she knew he had been.

Torn between fear and pain, she crouched low and ran through the tall grass toward the stream, hoping that if anyone saw her, they'd think she was some animal. Here the water was tumbling over artificial rapids. Willows trailed their thin branches in the current. Flopping down under their pale green curtain, she thrust wrist and ankle into the water. Gradually the sting was drawn out.

When she could notice something besides pain, Connie realized that the noise of falling water came from more than just this tame stretch of rapids. Was there a waterfall up ahead? Peering out from between drooping willow wands, she saw that a rocky cliff rose along the far side of the stream. Down its sheer face a second stream fell in a glittering cascade. Obviously, there wasn't a lot of choice about which stream to follow since she had never seen herself as a rock climber. But she did wish Rudy had been able to give her more complete directions.

She stood up. Just before this stream joined the second stream, it gurgled under a small humped bridge. On one side, the bridge led to an overgrown path, on the other, to a fantastic red-and-gold pagoda, with five roofs, each with upturned eaves, piled on top of each other like impossible hats. Seeing the questionable looking weeds clumped around its base, Connie skirted widely around it.

Trudging now up a steadily rising slope, Connie suddenly flattened herself into the grass. A car was driving on a distant, unseen road. She heard no other sound except the thumping of her own heart and some strange uncarlike honking from over the rise ahead. Nervously she crept on a little farther and realized the latest noise had come from geese, or were they swans? White shapes were humped along the shore of a small lake. Then one got up awkwardly, waddled toward the water, and glided out onto its surface. A swan.

But more importantly, a lake, and a lake with an island. Crouching down in the tall grass, she surveyed what must be her goal. It seemed, however, that beyond the one island was another and perhaps the tip of a third. She needed a better look at all of them. As she crept toward the water, the other white shapes got up and with a few indignant honks stalked there ahead of her.

But Connie wasn't as interested in the wildlife as in the islands. One held a little white temple like the top of a wedding cake. The next seemed to be the home of a naked stone lady—Venus or somebody. To see the third island well, she had to move farther along the shore, but there the grass had been replaced by mud and she felt awfully exposed. The stone walls of the castle were rising ominously close behind a thin screen of trees. Still, there didn't seem to be many windows on this side, though it felt as if a pair of hostile eyes were staring out of every dark narrow slit.

What if there was no grotto on this island? she wondered as she scuttled along. For that matter, what if there was? If she went there, would she be able to see something that would give her a clue as to where Rudy was? Maybe that was it.

However, when she finally got a good look at the third island through the branches of a low flowering bush, she could see it had neither grotto nor gargoyle. Instead there was the statue of a deer, the kind some people had for lawn ornaments back home. But from it's greeny-gold color, she decided that this one must be made of bronze instead of cement.

So what now?

The question fled. Two men were talking in voices that came steadily closer. Frantically she looked for a hiding place. There was a tall hedge of dark shiny holly, but it was from that direction that the voices were coming. Like a trapped deer, she wanted to run. But there was nowhere to hide.

CHAPTER

11

In desperation, Connie slipped into the lake itself. Ducking beneath the surface, she swam through the cold murky water toward a stand of reeds. She popped her head up again and found herself thinly screened from the shore by the rattling stalks of cattails.

Through them, she could see two men in uniform rounding the end of the hedge. They sauntered toward a stone bench halfway to the lake shore. Then settling down, one plunked a sack between them and pulled out two bottles of beer, several rolls, and some cheese.

"So, Hans," one said, "got any better idea of who this mysterious prisoner of ours is?"

"No, and I don't want to. Something tells me this is the sort of operation we're better off knowing as little about as possible."

"Come now, where's your curiosity? You'll never get promoted without showing some spark of initiative."

"And I'll be demoted to eternal janitorial duty or worse if I stick my nose where it's clearly not wanted. Spies, business deals, politics—it's all the same to me as long as I keep getting my orders and my paychecks. Where is the cheese knife?"

Connie wondered if she should try to hear more or try to get away. Through the reeds she caught a glint of metal, a gun hanging at the waist of one of the soldiers. Scrunching down to eye-level with the surface, she began paddling slowly backward through the reeds. She almost screamed when a water snake rippled past her nose. But it ignored her. Tiny frogs, however, did not and hopped out of her way as if on springs. She hoped the two soldiers couldn't hear the tiny ploppings all around her.

The water among the reeds was brown, motionless, and smelled slightly rotten. But as she moved farther into the lake, she could feel a faint current. Water had to feed into the lake from somewhere. And that could be her way out.

The guards' voices grew fainter as she paddled through the water following the hint of current. She imagined herself looking like an otter, its tiny smooth head leaving a V-shaped ripple behind it. If anyone saw her, she hoped they'd imagine the same. At least her dog paddle fit the picture. She liked swimming almost as much as running, but her parents had been afraid to let her do much of it.

At last she saw what she'd hoped for, a wedge of

open water cutting back into the reeds. She slid toward it until her feet touched the oozy mud of the lake bottom. Better not think about her recently new shoes. She knew her purse, bobbing on its strap behind her, was ruined.

The channel finally led to the mouth of a stream where the murky footing gave way to a stone-lined streambed and the steady flow of crystal water. Hidden by what was nearly a tunnel of overgrown bushes, Connie stood up and let the water flow off her like off a bird dog. If she'd had the energy, she would have shaken like a dog too. Hitching her sodden purse more securely over her shoulder, she squeezed some water from her long braid, took a step forward, and fell on her face.

Palms pressed painfully against the stones of the streambed, she stared dizzily through the water gurgling a few inches from her nose. She saw not only the water-worn cobbles, but also the coarse square-cut stones of a wall, the wall of the tower room.

Slowly she managed to stand up again, and both images held. Then a chessboard came into sight. Rudy was playing chess with one of his guards, but maybe he'd also been concentrating on her while she'd been thinking only of getting out of that lake. Now he moved a chess piece as she took a cautious step. She didn't fall. Then she took another and another. It could be practice, or the fact that they were very close now, but the dizziness seemed less overpowering.

Crouching beneath the crisscrossed arch of bushes, she walked cautiously up the little stream. All the while, the ghostly chess game continued before her. She was now almost right beneath the castle walls, but here its brooding stone presence was largely screened by a curtain of poplar and blue spruce. After what seemed an eternity of bending over, the tunnel of greenery gave way and she found herself staring into the mouth of a cave partially screened by hanging vines. The grotto?

"Way to go! " Rudy suddenly exclaimed.

His chess opponent lowered the piece he was holding. "You want me to make that move?"

"Oh, no, sorry. I was just thinking of something else. Another move I could make."

More confident now, Connie walked forward. She was able to sort of push the tower scene to the background and concentrate on the one actually before her. This might be the grotto, but its inhabitants weren't gargoyles, they were mermaids.

There were three of them, their scaly tails and human bodies all of green-gold bronze. From their seat on a real rock, two of them reached for what the third held playfully above her head, a bronze seashell. Out of it poured a steady ribbon of water that splashed over their sleek bodies and into the pool around them. From there the water flowed over the rocky edge and into the stream that fed the lake.

Connie wanted to spend a lot more time with the

statues. She loved mermaids. But they were hardly gargoyles. Discouraged, she looked around. This was a bigger grotto than that one in Durstadt, but the mermaids were the only statues here.

No, wait. Something seemed to be carved in the rock wall way in the back. Scrambling over mossy stones, Connie looked closer. The light back there was dim and green, but the figure it showed was no mermaid. A hunched body, grotesque face, and snarling mouth. Definitely a gargoyle. Boy, had that Gustav been weird, she thought. He'd put these nasty creatures all over.

What was it Charlotte had said when she and Rudy were playing hide-and-seek? She had already discovered what Rudy thought only he knew, that every gargoyle in the Durstadt palace guarded some secret. Connie smiled. The same secret?

She looked at the stone creature intently. The one by the library fireplace had worked when Rudy pulled its ear. But this one didn't have anything on top of its head but a tangle of stone hair. It did, however, have bulging eyes and a rudely dangling tongue.

Timidly she reached for the tongue and grabbed it. It felt cold and gross, but she gave it a jerk, wobbling it slightly. Another tug and it shifted to the right. With all her strength, she shoved it to the side of the mouth. Beside her, what had appeared to be a solid pillar of stone shuddered and, with a rough grinding sound, swung outward. A narrow shaft of darkness appeared beyond.

"Good move!" Rudy said, and abruptly the image of a chessboard appeared more vividly against Connie's stone doorway. Resolutely she walked through the vision and entered the dark cleft.

"Yes, it was good, wasn't it?" the guard replied. "You know, Your Highness, if the king and queen do ransom you, I'm going to miss these games. No one else properly appreciates my strategic style."

Scarcely listening to the talk of chess, Connie concentrated on climbing the rough stairs she'd found beyond the opening. They were dimly lit by an occasional crack in the stone wall. After a while the natural stone gave way to cut blocks, and she realized she must have come up from under the castle and was now inside one of the castle walls. Light now came from regularly placed slits, but it did little to illuminate the stairs or the crunching layer of trash that littered them. Connie was just as glad. She'd rather not know for sure that she was walking on bird bones and dried up old mouse bodies. She didn't imagine people had used this passage for years, except perhaps visiting princes who were bent on exploring.

Suddenly the stairs ended in a blank wall. She felt its surface. No gargoyle, nothing. How was she going to . . .

Her fingers scraped something metal. A big iron

ring set into the stone. She pulled at it gingerly, then braced her feet and tugged.

With a sound like an opening tomb, a stone door inched toward her. Another tug and she had a gap big enough to slip through.

She found herself in a small, almost circular, room. Its bare stone walls were lit by the afternoon sun streaming through a narrow window of stained glass. Blues and reds and greens splashed in vibrant pools on the flagstone floor.

Blinking in the light, Connie looked around. A set of spiral stairs rose from the shadows at the windowless end of the room. She started toward it then stopped.

Hadn't Rudy said something about a lion tapestry being in the room at the bottom of his stairs? Nothing was on the walls here except a rather gloomy painting of a man in a helmet. And she knew there were a number of round towers in the castle, all probably holding spiral stairs. Better look for another.

There were two doors out of the room. From beyond one she could hear distant voices, too far off to make out words, but their very presence was a threat. She headed for the other door.

"Wrong!" Rudy said firmly.

"What's wrong?" his opponent said with a startled frown.

"Oh, sorry. I was thinking of my next move and

decided it was the wrong one. I'm afraid I talk to myself rather a lot."

"Hmm, well, most folks do. And frankly, Your Highness, you don't seem nearly as nutsy as rumor has it."

Rudy looked at him a moment then shrugged. "Yeah. Rumors sure can exaggerate things. I just have dizzy spells and pass out occasionally. But I'm not possessed by demons or anything."

The guard nodded. In a room somewhere below, Connie smiled. No, not by demons exactly.

Clearly then, she had to go the direction from which the voices came. Every muscle tensed to run, she creaked open the door. The room she looked into was long and narrow with leaded glass windows and tapestries on the wall. At the far end, two people were standing, staring toward her. She almost slammed the door when she realized they were suits of armor. She continued her examination. A fireplace crouched cold and dark against one wall, and above it hung a huge painting of a fat man on a horse pointing with his sword. Connie supposed he was trying to look heroic, but he'd only managed to look silly.

At the far end of the room, between the empty suits of armor, was another closed door. Silent as a ghost, Connie ran over the dark patterned carpet toward it. The sound of voices seemed nearer.

Leaning fearfully against the door, she listened.

It didn't sound as if people were talking in the next room. Cautiously she peered in. This room didn't seem as ancient as the last. Everything was grander, lighter, and fussier. Every few yards along one wall, windows ran from floor to ceiling, and between them were tall gold-framed mirrors. Lined up along the other wall, tautly upholstered chairs and couches perched on delicate gold legs. Hardly an arrangement to encourage friendly chatting.

She was tiptoeing down the white-and-gold carpet when suddenly the voices seemed to be almost in the room. In a panic, she dropped to the floor and rolled under one of the high couches. She felt as conspicuous as a pig at a fashion show, but the two men striding into the room didn't notice her.

"Yes, *mein Herr*," one man said in a groveling tone. "The cars are ready and so is the helicopter. However things turn out, we can all be out of here in minutes."

The other man stopped and turned to the first. "Joseph, you needn't say 'however things turn out.' We will succeed. My part in the new government will not be inconsiderable, and I have every intention of enjoying it. But I want to be sure that when the time comes we are ready to move."

They started walking again, and Connie tried to get a look at something other than their feet. Finally she saw their reflections in one of the mirrors. Neither was familiar. The man in charge certainly wasn't Uncle

Albrecht, but he hadn't been talking like he was the top dog either. Maybe he was the current Baron von Himmelstein.

They cut across the carpet, heading for a different door from the one Connie had used. The first man was speaking again. "Naturally we will succeed, but as you always say, it is best to plan for contingencies."

"Exactly. And remember, Joseph, if our *guest* does have to be disposed of, that contingency is your responsibility."

"Naturally, naturally, *mein Herr*. All has been arranged."

The men passed from the room, and Connie found herself shivering, and it wasn't just that she was cold and wet. Alarmed at that thought, she looked at the pale carpet she'd just rolled over, but there was no trail of swamp water. She guessed her clothes had pretty well drip-dried in that awful passage.

Clearly, her choices were becoming fewer. Somehow she had to get Rudy out of this place. "Disposed of," they'd said. She shivered again, crawled from under the couch, and sprinted toward the far door.

The next two rooms were smaller but similar to the last. Magnificent mirrors and chandeliers, and lots of formally arranged, uncomfortable-looking furniture. Their walls of white, pink, or pale blue were lavishly trimmed in gold. Then she passed through another door and seemed to be in an older part of the castle again.

Narrow windows were set in thick stone walls. Of the three doors that led out of the room, one appeared to go to the outside. Before she could examine the others, she noticed the flight of stone stairs spiraling up from the far end of the room. On one wall hung a smallish tapestry featuring an animal that looked like a pig wearing a wig. Probably the artist had never seen a real lion.

Connie looked at the base of the stairs and knew they were the same ones she had seen days earlier. Rudy had been dragged in through that door, the tape wrenched off his eyes, and then been pushed up these winding stone stairs. He had known where he was because he had come to this castle before. Now she knew because she had seen it through his eyes while a quarter of a planet away.

So now that she was here, what was she going to do? She guessed Rudy was thinking of the problem too, because he had just lost his chess game miserably.

"I'm sorry, Michael," he said to his guard. "I wasn't a very worthy opponent this time. Guess my mind was elsewhere."

"Yes, I imagine so," Michael said, standing up and stretching. Connie could see the bulge of a gun in his pocket.

"Yes, but it isn't just that," Rudy said standing up and walking to the window. "It's the rats."

"Rats?"

140

"Yes. Big ones, vicious ones. Haven't you heard them?"

"I haven't heard anything." The voice sounded a little squeaky.

"Well, maybe not on your usual shift, and the other guards probably didn't tell you. But this castle and grounds are infested with giant rats. Always have been. We used to come here for visits when I was a kid. The place was better kept up then, but even so the rats were a menace. I was attacked by them once." He shuddered dramatically. "I still have the scars on my legs."

Leaning against the fireplace, Michael looked pale despite his skeptical smile. "So you think that once having had a taste of your royal blood, they'll be back for more?"

"No, I don't think they're particular. But they smell people trapped in here, I think. Sometimes at night, and even in late afternoon, I hear them scratching in the walls and under the door. They do have sharp claws. I keep worrying they'll get in."

Michael laughed, a little nervously it seemed. "Don't worry, my Prince. I shall defend you to the end against the giant Himmelstein rats."

"Good to hear it," Rudy said. His back to the guard, he was making scratching motions with one hand. But Connie didn't need any more hints, she was already starting up the stairs. Then she stopped and

141

looked around. Her eye fell again on the lion tapestry. Quietly she slipped back down and with some difficulty lifted it off the wall.

Clutching the wadded up tapestry, Connie crept up the winding stairs. One round, then two, then three. The vistas through the window slots were just as she had seen them. Only then it had been early morning and now it was late afternoon.

Finally she was standing on the uppermost landing. She had managed to control the dizziness pretty well on the way up, but now it hit with almost full force. Rudy was on the other side of that wooden door, and she was suddenly very aware of seeing two sides of it at once.

Swaying for a minute, she fought to keep hold of her own view and not its reverse. Slowly she gained control again. Then spying a wooden stool against one wall, she dropped her tapestry, quietly picked up the stool, and moved it to a spot just beyond where the door would open. Finally she got down on her hands and knees and began scratching.

Seeing herself scratching on one side of the door while at the same time seeing the reaction on the other, it was hard to keep from giggling.

Michael dropped the magazine he was reading and stiffened. Rudy stared up at him, trying to look innocent and frightened. Then he got up out of his chair and backed away from the door.

Connie stopped scratching, made some loud sniffing noises, then started scratching at another part of the door. Through Rudy's eyes, she could see the guard inching toward the door while Rudy slowly circled around behind him. She saw the guard reach into a pocket and pull out his gun. As he tiptoed toward the door, his back was to the prince. Quickly Rudy reached down and picked up a stout stick of firewood.

The guard's hand was closing on the doorknob. Connie stopped her scratching, grabbed up the tapestry, and climbed onto the stool.

With a rush the guard turned the lock and flung open the door. Connie dropped the tapestry like a sack over his head. Blindly the man waved his gun and fired once. The bullet pinged into a stone wall. His muffled yell was cut short by Rudy cracking the log down on his head.

Rudy and Connie exchanged shocked grins. Together they dragged the guard back into the room, stepped out, and locked the door. Then they pelted down the stairs. Already they could hear distant shouts. The gunshot had not gone unnoticed.

Their double vision seemed to have faded, and each now looked out of only one set of eyes. But speeding down these spiral steps left them almost as dizzy.

They had just staggered to the bottom when three men burst in through the outside door and stood staring at them. The one with the handlebar mustache held a gun.

CHAPTER

12

For a second Connie just stared at the man with the gun. Then Rudy grabbed her arm and pulled her after him through another door behind the stairs.

This wasn't a room Connie had been through, though it looked vaguely familiar. A library, she decided, as she rushed past the walls lined with books. They burst through the door at the far end just as their pursuers burst through the one behind.

"Stop!" the man with the mustache called. He punctuated his order with a gunshot. Terrified, Connie slammed the door behind them and flicked down the lock.

"Look out!" Rudy yelled. She looked up to see a knight lunging toward her. She leaped aside as the empty suit of armor crashed into a heap, further blocking the doorway.

"Always wanted to do that." Rudy called as they sped through that room and into the next. After two more small rooms, they entered an elegant salon with tall French windows. Rudy ran to one and after fumbling with the lock, flung it open onto a wide terrace.

Connie was expecting to follow him out, but he swerved back into the room whispering "Follow Me!" Halfway across the rug, they heard footsteps drumming toward them, and crouched down behind a grand piano. Peering past its carved legs, they saw the legs of the three men dash in, hesitate a moment, then rush out the open French window onto the terrace.

From outside a voice called, "Turn out everybody to search for them. It's not easy to get out of these grounds."

Crablike, Rudy and Connie scuttled over the wine-red carpet and through a door into yet another room. Again they were running, with Connie wondering if they'd ever find their way out of this maze. Abruptly, they turned a corner into a narrow hall and ran smack into an old man carrying a stack of linen. The sheets flew into the air, then settled around him in a heap.

Before they could sidle past, the old man gripped Rudy's shoulder. Angrily he opened his mouth, but the scolding words sputtered away. He squinted at the boy.

"Your Highness? Prince Rudolph?"

"Yes. Alfred, is it? Good to see you, but I'm sorry I can't stop to chat."

The other just kept staring. "But why are you here, Your Highness. We were told . . ."

"Actually, I'm running away from someone just now. Someone with a gun. Alfred, if you have any loyalty to my family, *please* don't tell anyone you've seen me."

Before the old man could stutter out his loyalty, Rudy and Connie were past him and off down the hall again. They dashed through a storeroom and were suddenly at the foot of another flight of spiral stairs. It was the first castle room Connie had entered. A thin crack of black in one of the walls showed where she hadn't pulled the secret door all the way to.

Soon they had done so, but from the safety of the other side. As the silence and musty darkness settled around them, Connie leaned against the wall and let her trembling knees lower her to the ground.

Rudy did the same, then he chuckled. "Nice seeing you again, Connie."

"Sure. Any time I can be of service, don't hesitate to call."

When they'd finished their hushed laughter, Rudy said, "Where's Wolfie gone? Surely he's not letting you have all the fun on your own."

"He's in some hospital."

"What?"

"These guys are really serious, Rudy. They not only tried to blow us up at the airport, they deliberately ran Wolfie down when he was crossing a street."

146

"Wolfie! Is he okay?"

"Keep your voice down. These walls aren't *that* thick. He didn't seem too awfully smashed up. He was able to tell me to hide so they wouldn't get me too. But I was the only one who had any idea where you were, and we hadn't been able to get through to the palace. A lot of people seem to be in on this plot."

"Are my parents okay? I don't know what's been happening, trapped in that tower like some fairy-tale princess."

"With a humble commoner rescuing you. As far as I know, they are fine. The kidnappers' demands were to change some government policies and to change the line of succession probably in favor of Uncle Albrecht."

"Figures. Baron von Himmelstein is an old buddy of his. Which makes me think we'd better get moving."

"Wouldn't we be better off staying in here until it gets dark outside?"

"Maybe. But if the baron is around . . ."

"I think I saw him earlier."

"Then let's move. After all, he grew up in this place and probably knows a lot more of the secret passages than I've found. If they decide that open door trick was fake, they might poke around inside some more."

"Right."

Hastily they descended the dark litter-strewn stairs until they reached the back of the grotto. Low sunlight was filtering through the curtain of hanging vines, giving everything a misty green cast.

Rudy looked around. "It certainly has grown over since I was here last. How'd you ever find it from just that drawing I did?"

"I didn't. I found the lake all right, but it had three islands not one and none of them had grottos or gargoyles. Then I sort of stumbled on this place while trying to sneak away from a couple of soldiers."

"Hey, that circle and dot wasn't a lake with one island, it was a gargoyle inside a cave."

"Great! Well, anyway, I remembered about Gustav's gargoyles."

Walking past the playful mermaids, Rudy peered out through cascading vines. "How did you get into the grounds? That fellow was right, it's not easy."

Connie smiled. "I fell in with some local berry thieves who showed me a way through, where the fence crosses the stream. Then I took what must be the long way around, past a pagoda and a ruined minicathedral. Is there a more direct way?"

"Sure, follow me."

They parted the vines and looked out over a calm peaceful scene. In the west, the sun was near to setting. Streaming away from it, the shadows of trees and bushes spilled across the rolling lawns. Nearer by, reeds rustled in a cool evening breeze and through them they could glimpse flashes of silver from the placid expanse of lake. Rudy turned to the left and forged a path

148

through the carpet of ferns at the base of a stony bluff.

They emerged from the ferns and scented pines to an open grassy swatch around the lake, but on the opposite shore from the one Connie had approached. There was very little cover.

Kneeling in the shaggy grass, Rudy pointed to a grove of wind-twisted cyprus. "There's a shortcut down to the main stream on a stairway starting from those trees."

Crouching low, they ran toward the trees. Suddenly the breeze-ruffled silence erupted into a flurry of honking and of flapping wings. They had charged into a clump of napping swans. Most fluttered skyward or bolted toward the water, but one deliberately charged after them, hissing and snapping its beak. Connie thought the avenging swan was scary enough until she heard men shouting on the far side of the lake.

"There! Across the lake. Get them!"

Swerving away from the demented swan, they redoubled their speed only to find themselves at the edge of a cliff. To their left, the ground sloped sharply away under a cascade of dark shiny green ivy.

Skidding to a halt, they scanned the precipice for a way down. "Nope," Rudy said. "We need those stairs."

As they turned around, gunfire cut through the air. Startled, Connie stepped back, lost her balance, and with flailing arms began teetering over the edge. Rudy lunged for her just as she fell. With a jarring thud, they both landed on the steep slope and began sliding wildly down its ivy-slicked surface. Frantically they grabbed at vines only to have them tear out by the roots. But at least this slowed their progress so that when they landed in the wild rose bushes at the base of the cliff, they were only slashed by thorns and not broken into bits.

When he staggered free of the bushes, Rudy gasped, "Quicker than stairs, anyway. Now for the falls."

Examining herself for broken bones, Connie watched skeptically as Rudy hobbled to the upper stream and began wading down it. From the crashing gurgle in the air, the falls were clearly not far ahead. "Hey," she said, hurrying after him. "I don't like doing my own stunts. No going over waterfalls!"

Rudy just trudged ahead, and with large rocks closing in, Connie had to follow him into the stream. They were nearly at the rim of the falls, with the current tugging hungrily at their ankles, when Rudy reached up to an overhanging rock and pulled himself out. Gratefully Connie did the same.

They'd no sooner crouched behind a mossy boulder than they heard voices from above. "They're down there somewhere. Come on, the stairs are over here."

Rudy tugged Connie's arm and began scrambling down a narrow path alongside the falls. At least, it must have once been a path. Half the stones that bordered it had fallen away, and the remaining track was slick with mud or spongy green moss. Connie decided that just throwing herself over the falls might have been safer after all.

When they'd finally stumbled and slid to the bottom, Rudy pointed across the little humpbacked bridge to the pagoda.

"Don't tell me you know a secret passage from there," Connie said.

"No, sorry. But if we get there in time, there're good hiding places. When we played hide-and-seek, even Baron von Himmelstein's nasty daughter couldn't find me there."

When they'd crossed the bridge and climbed up the stone platform, none of their pursuers were yet in sight. Rudy scrambled up on one of the stone lions that crouched at the base of a wooden column. Then clutching a carved snake head, he pulled himself up into the coils that entwined the pillar. From there it was a short scramble up to the elaborately carved eaves of the roof.

Connie definitely did not want to follow him. But she wanted even less to be caught here in the open-sided pagoda. Not letting herself think, she climbed from lion to snake to entwining grilles. She made her way farther up into the intricate woodwork, then jamming her hands and feet into gaps the way Rudy had, she hung on like a bat or, she thought, like some new demonic carving. She hoped if the men came this way, they wouldn't be too curious about the artwork. She could always stick out her tongue like the carved dragon next to her, but she wasn't covered with the same peeling red-and-gold paint.

Within minutes two men who had obviously taken an easier route were indeed standing on the raised platform of the pagoda. They scanned the sweep of lawns, trees, and romantic ruins. Sunset had turned the sky a soft peach color. Reflecting its glow, the stream cut through the darkened grass like a festive ribbon.

"It'll be too dark soon to hunt for them," one of the men said. "Let's go back and have Himmelstein send for some hounds. They can trail the little brats anywhere."

When the two were out of sight, Connie looked over to where Rudy seemed to have comfortably blended himself into the carvings. "Can we get down now, do you think?"

"No," he whispered back. "There still might be others looking around. We'd better wait till it's dark."

"What about the hounds?"

"Himmelstein doesn't have any hounds. At least he didn't. He'll have to send for some. It'll take time."

Connie was silent a minute then asked, "Have you come here often? I never remember being with you when you did."

"No, we didn't come often, and then only for a few days at a time, but when we did come, I went wild exploring. There was one visit though when it rained all the time. You did visit me then, I seem to remember, but I spent most of my time in the library. I was pretty little then."

Connie nodded, though the gesture could scarcely be seen in the growing dusk. That explained why the library and a few of the other rooms had seemed slightly familiar.

After a while she said, "You know, this is just the sort of thing my mother would never let me do. Climb up something high and difficult to get down from. Always worried about what would happen if I had one of my spells."

"They wouldn't have let me either, if they'd known. But I doubt there's any danger now. I don't think we'll have regular passing out type spells when we're this close."

"I guess that means if we want to be perfectly normal all the time we have to stick together."

"I've heard worse ideas," he replied.

Connie wasn't sure if he was joking or serious, but then another definitely worse idea crossed her mind. "Rudy, why do you think they were shooting at you? Surely if they killed you, that would wreck their scheme."

"Hmm. Maybe. But I'm not sure they were shooting at *me*."

Connie felt cold. "But why would they shoot me? I don't mean anything to them."

"No, but clearly you do to me. If you'd been shot,

I would have stopped to help. Then they would have had me just the same."

After a minute's silence, Connie said in a smallish voice, "I know travel is supposed to be broadening, but I don't care for the way things are done around here. Let's get down; if we wait much longer I won't be able to see that easy little route we took up here."

"It's dark up here under the eaves, all right. But down on the grass we'd still stand out."

She looked doubtfully down at the carved snake dimly coiling up the column. "Yeah, but the baron might have hounds someplace near."

"True. Well, it's nearly dark enough. Let's go."

Once Rudy was down, Connie looked at him standing way below on the stone platform and doubted that she could ever manage to climb down. She'd be stuck up there forever, a skeleton blending into the other creepy carvings.

The soft evening breeze, however, suddenly brought her motivation: The faint baying of hounds.

CHAPTER
13

Almost without realizing how she'd done it, Connie was standing beside Rudy at the base of the pagoda. Again they heard the distant baying of hounds, and together they shot over the grass like hunted deer.

Connie took the lead now. The rolling waves of lawn looked as dark and unreal as smoke. Above them in the west, a crescent moon cast only the thinnest silver light over the scene.

They ran along the course of the stream. The ruins of the strange miniature cathedral loomed darkly on their right, its arches splayed like bare bones against the sky. Then it passed, and there were only mournful clumps of poplars and pines whispering and swaying in the cool breeze. The breeze also carried the sound of hounds, louder and clearer than before.

"How much farther?" Rudy gasped as he thumped over the ground behind her.

"Almost there. Where the bushes crowd the water, we use the stream."

"Good. It'll throw them off the scent."

But it proved slow going, running in the stream. The water seemed thick and heavy, and the smooth mossy cobbles were uneven and slipped under foot. Often the two lost their balance and splashed totally into the water.

"Those hounds won't need scent," Rudy sputtered as he rose from a dunking. "They'll just hear us."

Suddenly they were at the fence. Crouching down, Connie slipped under it, tearing her mud-stained blouse on the jagged wire. Rudy followed, and after clearing the brambles they scrambled out onto the bank.

"Well," Rudy said between gasps, "where to now?"

Connie hadn't thought much beyond this point, as though once free of the ogre's castle some wicked enchantment would be broken. But she could still hear the hounds, and they sounded much nearer.

"If we could get to the village," she offered, "there should be people about and police maybe."

"Whose side'll they be on?"

"Hey, you're their prince. They won't want to see you torn apart by dogs."

"Me neither," Rudy said, scrambling after her.

Connie wasn't at all sure she could find the path Otto had led her down earlier, but when she stopped thinking about it, her legs seemed to find it on their own. Soon they were climbing steadily upward, and through the trees they could see the glimmer of a few house lights.

Behind them came the chorus of dogs added to by several human voices. The pack must almost have reached the fence, Connie thought as she struggled desperately upward. Ahead, some of the village dogs were joining in the ruckus. Among them, she couldn't miss Heidi's kettle-drum barking. And it wasn't coming from far away.

Looking back, Connie thought she glimpsed dark shapes dashing through the trees. The hounds were through. They were almost upon them!

With fear-renewed speed, she crashed into the backyard of the Müllers' house, but she didn't go in. Instead, she ran to Heidi's pen where the huge Great Dane was now hurling herself against the chain link fence barking terribly to get out.

"Good girl, Heidi," Connie called above the noise. "Give us a hand, will you?" Fumbling with the catch, she threw open the gate.

Rudy shrank back against her as the great black dog bounded past them. "What was that?"

"A friend. Let's get into the village."

The lights in the Müllers' house had switched on, but Connie didn't want to drag them into danger. Their pursuers probably weren't above shooting innocent bystanders. Running through the side yard, they burst out onto the road and sped along it past a growing number of houses until they reached the village square. The street lights were on, a few people were still walking about, and there were even some cars.

Exhausted, Rudy and Connie sank down at the foot of the village's stone cross and struggled to catch their breath. A few people stared curiously at the two wet, disheveled young people, and received faint relieved smiles in return. It felt as if they'd reached sanctuary at last.

Behind them, way down the lane they could still hear dogs, but it no longer sounded like a pack in pursuit. It sounded like a first-class dogfight. Two new dogs, a dachshund and a large shaggy mutt came trotting across the village square, eager to join in.

Rudy grunted and wearily rose to his feet. "Looks like we've made their day. But much as I'd like to just curl up like a dog right here, we'd better get inside somewhere. If I could figure out who it'd be safe to phone, I'd do it. Surely the local police wouldn't be in on this plot. Maybe we . . ."

His voice trailed off as he focused on a dark green car that had just driven into the square and pulled up between themselves and the one open restaurant.

Both of their hearts seemed to freeze in midbeat. Baron von Himmelstein sat behind the wheel.

CHAPTER 14

The baron gave the children a gracious smile while two men stepped from the car and moved toward them. One had a large black mustache, the other a blond crew cut. They both held guns.

"I am so sorry," the baron said, "that my hospitality did not seem to suit Your Highness. But perhaps you will give me a second chance. Do, please, get in."

Connie and Rudy looked hopelessly at each other, then before they could move a muscle, the two men had grabbed their arms and yanked them into the backseat. Coarse, musty smelling sacks were pulled over their heads and the car sped off.

The smell of the sack, the jolting ride, and the incredible disappointment, made Connie nearly ill. It had all been for nothing. Now they'd both be prisoners in that awful castle, and nobody would know they were there, let alone get them out.

Connie gave up even trying to sense direction as they rumbled along, but then they turned from the paved road and jolted up what felt like a steep rutted farm track. Finally they pulled to a halt.

The two children were hauled out, and the sack was yanked off Connie's head. She breathed in deep lungfuls of fresh night air and groggily looked around. They and the car stood on the edge of an open field. A thick belt of trees dropped away steeply on one side. On the other, a strange monstrous shape squatted in the darkness. She stared at it and slowly realized it was a helicopter. Suddenly the baron was standing in front of her.

"I have no idea, young lady, how you fit into this. But I intend to learn. The usefulness of your companion, however, seems to have come to an end."

"You can't . . ."

"No speeches, please. We can and will. From what we have just learned, it seems that all has not gone as planned in Durstadt. So I and several of my companions need to make a quick trip across the border. But first . . ."

Turning to the man with the mustache, he ordered, "You help get the chopper ready. And you," he said pointing at Crew Cut, "you may prepare for the honor of being a royal firing squad."

Connie watched in horror. Rudy's hands were bound together in front of him, the sack over his head was tightened, and he was dragged stumbling to the edge of the forested ravine. Then Crew Cut strolled away a few steps, leaned against a tree and began toying with his gun.

"Of course," the baron said calmly to Connie, "if you tell me by what channels you learned of our plans, I might spare you."

Connie stood confused and silent. A smile flicked around the baron's lips. "I might even spare the fabulous fainting prince here. You see, I am not unreasonable."

Connie saw nothing of the sort. She knew they'd both be killed the moment she told him what he wanted to know—which she couldn't do anyway since he was expecting some complex story about her being a junior CIA agent or something. But there was one thing she did see.

Mustache Man had gone off to talk with the helicopter pilot, and the light from the cockpit had been switched on. By its watery glow she could clearly see that Crew Cut was standing just four feet to Rudy's right. If only Rudy didn't have that sack over his head, he could see how easy it would be to strike out at him. But he couldn't see.

"So," the baron continued, "how about telling me who your contacts are? You're obviously not an average American teenager. Why did Reichmann bring you back? How did you learn of our location?"

Connie wasn't paying attention to him. She was staring at Rudy, thinking about the fear and musty darkness that must be engulfing him now. Dizziness rose up around her, and she deliberately dove into it; it was like moving into a murky pool. Her own sight shimmered, then half-faded into the darkness of his.

Rudy swayed, then noticeably he straightened up. Could he now see things as she was seeing them?

While the baron talked on, Connie watched as Rudy, with seeming random restlessness, moved one, then two steps closer to his guard. She stared intently at the closing gap between them.

In a lightening move, Rudy swung his bound hands out and down on Crew Cut's gun. The man yelped and fumbled after the weapon as it skidded off into the bracken.

The baron spun around, and Connie bolted past him straight for Rudy. Grabbing his bound arms, she pulled him after her into the ravine. With her free hand, she yanked the sack off his head, then running and falling and scrambling up again, they crashed down the slope.

From above, shots were fired and orders yelled, but it sounded like nobody charging after them. Then before they had reached the bottom of the ravine, they heard the whirring clatter of a helicopter taking off. The two crouched behind a tumble of rotten logs. After the lights slashed a few times through the treetops, the machine veered off in the other direction. The direction of the nearest border.

*   *   *

162

Several minutes later, two dazed fourteen-year-olds, scratched, filthy, and incredibly relieved were trudging up a deserted Thulgarian highway. Stars glittered overhead in a narrow ribbon between the trees. The only sounds were their own tired footsteps, the rhythmic chirping of insects, and an occasional rustle or birdcall from the surrounding woods.

After half an hour's steady walking, there was a change. Cars were coming toward them. They could see the lights. Among the several headlights was a flashing multicolored beacon, like on the top of a police car. And there were sirens.

Both Connie and Rudy started to dive for cover among the roadside bushes, then Rudy said, "Wait a moment. Police or army. That's probably what we need. We're going to have to trust someone sometime. Let's see if we can flag them down."

Connie was too tired to argue. Running and hiding had become so much a habit, it just seemed the natural thing to do.

Like frozen deer, they stood beside the road staring at the oncoming lights. Then they began waving their arms. The lead motorcycles swept by, but the flashing police car pulled to the side and stopped.

The two walked over to it, and Rudy said through the open window, "Excuse me, officer, but we are in need of some official protection. You see . . ."

"Rudy! Is that you?"

Rudy spun around, and Connie followed his stare.

A man had just stepped from the car that had pulled up behind. A short slim man with gray hair and a strained expression on his bearded face.

"Papa!" they both called and ran toward him.

With a joyful cry, the king embraced his son. Then he turned a curious look on Connie, who was now shyly hanging back.

A second man stepped from the car behind the king. The flashing police light glinted off his glasses and highlighted the whiteness of the sling holding his arm.

"Wolfie!" Now it was Connie's turn to hug someone, though Rudy wasn't far behind. When he disengaged himself, Wolfie looked at the king. "This is Fraulein Constance, Your Majesty, the American girl of whom I told you, though how both of these missing persons should happen to be here, is something I can't begin to explain."

Then everyone began talking at once. Rudy managed to tell his father that the baron and a couple of his followers had escaped toward the border. But in the hopes of catching some of the others, the police were dispatched to the castle. Orders crackled back and forth over a radio. After a while Connie and Rudy stopped trying to listen to everything and just sagged against the side of a car.

Soon, however, things quieted down and they were bundled into the king's gray limousine. Connie found herself sitting on one side of the king with Rudy on the other. She supposed she ought to feel awkward, but she didn't. The sudden change in their immediate situation was dazzling, but sitting beside the king of Thulgaria seemed almost as normal and comforting as sitting beside her own father.

Smoothly, the car turned around and, with two motorcycles in attendance, headed back to Durstadt. Among the occupants, eager questions flew back and forth. Finally Connie got off one to Wolfie, who was sitting across from them in the limousine's backward-facing seat.

"How did you manage to get through to the palace from the hospital? Weren't you afraid the phones would be tapped?"

Wolfie gave an embarrassed chuckle. "I didn't use a telephone. I didn't even go to the hospital. Once I was in the ambulance and started getting my mind back together, I showed the attendants all my impressive identity papers and told them it was a matter of vital importance to the throne that I be taken directly to the palace. So we drove back to Durstadt and up to the palace itself. Nobody's going to stop a screaming ambulance. Then they threw me on a stretcher and took me right in to the king and queen."

Rudy whistled. "And all the while you had a broken arm and whatever else from being hit by that car."

"I guess the excitement carried me through. I didn't pass out until I'd told most of my story."

The king laughed. "And an incredible story it was too. Except that it all fit together. And right then, Catherine and I were ready to believe any craziness if it would help get Rudy back."

Rudy smiled up at his father, then asked, "How did you figure out where to go? It didn't sound as if Connie picked up very many useful clues from me, at least not until she'd left Wolfie."

"Well," the king answered, "it took us a while to piece everything together. But knowing we were looking for a castlelike building in the mountains about two hours from Durstadt, narrowed things down a little."

Wolfie joined in. "Then we got a map showing a grid of all the transmission towers. Connie's description suggested microwave rather than electrical or radio towers, so that narrowed it even further."

"Even so, there were still a number of possibilities," the king continued. "But among them, Himmelstein's castle rather stood out. Of late, the baron has become a good buddy of my dear trouble-making brother."

"Is Uncle Albrecht . . ." Rudy began.

"He should be under house arrest by now. We suspected his involvement right from the beginning, but he's not as clever a conspirator as he imagined, nor were all of his coconspirators as loyal to him as he thought. Just before we left Durstadt, the order was

166

issued to bring them all in, or as many as we knew of."

Sighing, the king looked at Rudy's drawn face. "Don't worry about Albrecht too much. He's ambitious and has mad ideas, but he's not an unmitigated villain. He was being manipulated by a lot of people with agendas of their own. And I do think he is sincerely fond of you and even concerned about your health." The king laughed mirthlessly. "Of course, he also may have been concerned that he couldn't influence your political thinking as easily as he'd hoped."

Rudy nodded, his expression relaxing some. "But what about General Herberhausen? Connie told me . . ."

"Yes, Herberhausen was in on it along with several others in the government and military. And it seems there were some foreign interests as well. We're still unraveling things, but apparently it wasn't as wide a conspiracy as we feared. We've been lucky."

The king shook his head and continued. "I'm afraid we have a good deal of political rethinking to do, domestically at least, and a fair amount of fence-mending. There may be room for more progressiveness without endangering our neutrality. But I am still convinced that most citizens of Thulgaria remain rather fond of their crown prince." He gave his son a cramped hug. "They're not likely to want him chucked out by a pack of plotters."

Rudy's look of happiness slid into a thoughtful one. "Do you think they'd still be as fond of me if they knew that what Albrecht said was sort of true? I'm not sickly or demented as he was apparently saying, but I'm not exactly normal. I do have some rather odd quirks." Leaning forward he looked at Connie and smiled. "Which I have no desire to be rid of."

The king looked serious. "Rudy, your mother and I have been talking about that, for months actually. We realize we have to be more forthright about things. A king can't lie to his people if he wants them to trust him. But maybe now that we have a better idea of what is happening . . ."

Both Connie and Rudy stiffened. "Papa," Rudy said, "I don't want a cure."

The king looked at the two beside him. Slowly he smiled. "No, I think if my problem were someone like Constance here, I wouldn't want a cure either. But maybe we can get a better understanding of what's happening now. Maybe some sort of control is possible."

He looked again at Connie. "You know, Constance my dear, it's hard to realize that if what Wolfgang says is true, you have been around us as long as my son has."

She smiled. "Yes, I guess it is hard, Your Majesty. Of course, we could start getting a little closer if you'd call me Connie. I hate Constance."

He laughed. "All right, Connie. Do you suppose

your parents would object if you stayed here with us for a while. We could even bring them over if they'd like. There are plenty of guest rooms in the palace. That way all those medical specialists who keep finding nothing could have a look at both of you."

Before either could object, he added, "I'm not talking about a cure here. I'm not sure that's possible, or even something we want. You two seem to be very special people. But I do think the time has come to learn what we're dealing with and how to handle it."

For a long moment, Connie and the prince looked at each other. Then both smiled.

"Yes," Connie said at last. "We could use learning more about a lot of things."

Rudy nodded. "Excuse the pun, but I suppose one could say we were of one mind on that."

The conversation buzzed on, and despite herself, Connie found her eyes closing. She'd settled comfortably against the king's warm shoulder and had almost drifted to sleep when a sudden thought bubbled to the surface pulling her with it.

"Rudy," she said leaning forward, "have you or your family ever run afoul of a witch?"

He looked perplexed. "Not that I know of. Why?"

"Oh, it's just that you seem to live in such interesting times."

Prince Rudolph laughed, then closed his eyes contentedly. "I guess one can put up with anything in moderation. Even interesting times."

169